Marcus Anthony Hunter attended Kent State University in Kent, Ohio. He was an actor and TV writer in Hollywood, California, from 1973 to 1980. *The Messenger* is his first published novel.

I dedicate this novel to my parents, Cecil and Marie Hunter, my brothers, Tim and Cecil Jr., my nephew, Tim Jr., and to my best friend and Hollywood star, Ernest L. Thomas.

Marcus Anthony Hunter

THE MESSENGER

AUSTIN MACAULEY PUBLISHERS™

LONDON * CAMBRIDGE * NEW YORK * SHARJAH

Ordering Information
Quantity sales: Special discounts are available on quantity purchases by corporations, associations, and others. For details, contact the publisher at the address below.

Publisher's Cataloging-in-Publication data
Hunter, Marcus Anthony
The Messenger

ISBN 9781645758945 (Paperback)
ISBN 9781645758938 (Hardback)
ISBN 9781645758952 (ePub e-book)

Library of Congress Control Number: 2020919896

www.austinmacauley.com/us

First Published (2021)
Austin Macauley Publishers LLC
40 Wall Street, 33rd Floor, Suite 3302
New York, NY 10005
USA

mail-usa@austinmacauley.com
+1 (646) 5125767

"I Gave the Lord My Soul"

A Gospel Poem
by
Marcus Anthony Hunter
and
Marie Moore Hunter

I gave the Lord my soul
I gave the Lord my heart
He's given me so much
I don't know where to start.

Once my soul was down and out
I'd lost hope and doubt
But one day, I fell down to my knees in prayer
I suddenly found the Lord everywhere.

I gave the Lord my soul
I gave the Lord my heart
He's given me so much
I don't know where to start.

By His stripes, I'm healed
By His love, I'm blessed
I thanked the Lord for his grace
For His word is forever written on my face.

Chapter 1
The Last Vacation

In one of the better-kept tracts of the greater Los Angeles area, the Metropolis, that had passed its golden years and stood on the brink of utter collapse, the Kelly family prepared for a rare and long-awaited weekend trip. Though most cities of the Los Angeles basin were run-down and rampant with crime due to massive unemployment, Pasadena remained one of the few surviving districts for the well to do.

Mrs. Ann Kellys, with her daughter following closely behind, got into a fairly old but well-kept 1987 Volkswagen Jetta which sat in the driveway. Charles Kellys leisurely took his time to lock the front door of his modest but stately looking two-story Brownstone home.

"Charles, did you remember to fill up?" Ann asked in a fidgety busy tone through the rolled-down window.

"Yes, I filled it to the brim early this morning," Charles answered laughing, acknowledging his wife's anxiousness.

The Kelly family couldn't find their way clear to go on vacation three times a year as was their custom in the past. Prices seemed to change so rapidly; higher and higher each month. But even with this, they still had nothing to complain about. Both were employed in comfortable stable jobs. He was a newsman for KGBII television and she a head nurse at the Los Angeles Medical Center. By every standard of an economically depressed and declining society, they were very well off.

"Okay, I guess we can go," Ann conceded, still getting the restless feeling that something had been forgotten. "Did you get the ice chest and the canvas bag off the kitchen table? You know the prices in those highway restaurants have gotten out of reach. I packed some of your favorite fruits in the bag, lots of cold drinks in the ice chest. I hope you remembered it. And don't forget Linda's radio-tape player. She can't go anywhere without music. This girl, I tell you, she's turning into a regular high stepper."

Charles was amused by the display of excitement being put on by his wife. She was behaving as if they had never been on a vacation before.

"Of course, dear. Yes, the food is sitting on the backseat floor under those blankets. Linda's radio is under the seat on my side. I even put a few rolls of paper towels in the trunk for the picnic. Something you forgot," Charles quipped with a smile.

After checking the loaded down car over for the last time, he spun his 170-pound frame into the front seat and casually, almost playfully, slipped the car keys out of his front pocket.

"Did you make sure all the windows were locked? Is the electric alarm system on? What about the double lock on the back door?"

Charles leaned over and looked at Ann who was glowing with anticipation. "Yes…yes…yes…don't be so nervous, honey, we've been on a vacation before. Don't worry, everything has been taken care of."

Starting up the car, Charles reversed out of the driveway, with his wife adjusting herself for comfort in the front seat, and Linda, his daughter, stretching out on the rear seat. As they pulled down the block, the Kellys waved to their neighbors, the Richardsons, who were returning home from work. He then sped off down the street, eastward. They were on their way to Desert Springs.

Upon reaching the Interstate Highway, Charles flipped on the cruise control. Energetic Linda had already turned on her radio. She drew up her knees and started to color farm scenery outlines with crayons from a large assorted box. The artistic strokes were made between body sways to the music. She was in her own private world.

After a seemingly endless chain of adjusting municipalities, they drove through miles of the countryside. Charles Kellys enjoyed the view. There were a few beer cans along the road here and there, and an inordinate number of trees had been cut down, but the view was still a nature relaxing green. Some of the horizons where the misty gray sky touched the ridges were, in a sense, breathtaking. Suddenly, Charles heard a thumping sound underneath the car. He noticed a truck pulling ahead of him, steeping up a broad incline, was losing much of its load on the highway. Charles had to swerve to miss another box, and then a loud flipping sound made him pull over to look under the car to see what the problem was.

He got out and saw a large piece of cardboard caught to the bottom of his car between the wheel and the fender well. Dislodging the obstruction from under the car, Charles got back in and slumped down in his seat.

"He ought to have that strapped down better," Charles commented before he started up the car again. "Either of you want anything? Linda, do you want something to drink? Need to use a restroom? Anything like that?"

Preoccupied in thought, Ann gazed out of the window. There were several minutes of silence because the disruption had broken the flow of what, up to now, had been a totally pleasant trip. Ann was cautioning at times, almost seeming superstitious, about mishaps. Something in her protective personality read disruptions as signs of what might lie ahead. She was often mistaken, but the times had gotten so bad that she was easily put on alert.

"Charles, maybe we shouldn't go this weekend," Ann said softly, looking over at him. "I get a funny feeling when things go wrong. That cardboard box could have been a sign."

"Don't worry, Ann," Charles said reassuringly. "We are going through with our plans. Tomorrow is not promised."

The open spaces appeared to widen out more the further Charles drove. The inclines took them higher in elevation, although the mountains were still miles away. Linda had a country and western tune blaring over the radio, deeply engrossed in the brown coloring of a big printed of a barn.

While she looked at the haze around, Ann shook her head in disgust. "Oh my God, you remember when we could see those mountains so clearly?"

"It's only clear now when it rains," Charles returned, "and it hasn't rained in over a year."

"Honey, can you actually remember the last time?" Ann quizzed.

"It has been so dry. And speaking of rain, you know it's been over a year since we've been able to drink the tap water," Charles added. "They keep telling us it's only a temporary problem, but nobody believes that. The region's water system has flat out broken down. Too dry, too much toxic seepage, too much pollution; the curing chemicals were overloading the system in volume and cost. With the bureaucratic red tape and palms being greased through payoffs; it could be another year before we get anything drinkable from those faucets. Were it not for our purification system, we probably couldn't even wash our clothes or even bath."

"I have read articles saying there have also been spot shortages of bottled water. This is really crazy. A lot of people on my job have taken to drinking more juice, brought in from out of state, preferably. The whole big city utility system is literally a mess. Whatever are we going to do?" Ann looked downward in genuine perplexity.

"I'm not sure. Most things are contaminated," Charles continued. "I got hold of a piece of news the other day that would be a real scandal if leaked to the public. The guy told me those so-called pure diet gardens that use deep spring water shipped in from Arkansas are actually using the same stuff we can't boil clean in L.A. That would mean the supposed healthy organic food overpriced in health food stores is tainted like our regular commercial variety."

"Charles…of course, you didn't believe him. Everyone isn't crooked. We still have some standards. That guy probably had an ax to grind with his supervisor or something."

"Anyway, I couldn't care what he said, that food is still better than some of the trash they have in the markets today. Why, I've seen some foods without a single bit of organic vegetable or mineral in them. All chemicals, totally artificial."

Ann surveyed the landscape again. Somehow, she didn't feel so bad. The futility of it all was so great that a person just felt helpless.

Charles approached a billboard advertising a souvenir shop. The pictorial display depicted a giant wigwam.

"Do you see the sign?" Ann shouted quickly to Linda. "Look! Look at the big Indian tent!"

Linda got a glance at it in excitement before they went by. Linda loved all Indian things. Her favorite doll, one of many which laid on her bedroom dresser, was the replica of an Indian squaw. Linda clapped her hands and smiled broadly, patting her mother on the shoulder.

"I'm getting hungry," Ann said, reaching behind her seat into the canvas bag. "You want an apple?"

"Sure," Charles answered with a smile.

Linda nodded affirmatively in agreement. Moments later, Ann pressed a handkerchief polished apple into her hand. She then gave one to Charles.

"Poly-sorbate, glycol-glycerin, ascorbyl-phosphate, and red dye number two…soon, man will be able to reproduce this apple with nothing but chemicals," Charles joked.

Ann toyed with Charles's thought, "Maybe they already have." She waved her hand over Charles's apple and shook it lightly as if casting a spell.

"Wooo…this apple tastes kinda funny. Look at it when you bite into it. It has no seeds. No stem. Augggh! Look, Charles, that red! It's all over you, you'll never get it off! Lookout, Charles…it's spreading…it's coming to get me! Ah, a-a-a!" Ann pretended a choking attack by jokingly grabbing at her throat.

Charles was amused by the little drama played out.

"Stop it," Charles choked out in a laugh. "I can't keep my eye on the road!"

"The apples," Ann jokingly continued, "They're gonna get us all!"

"Come on, honey. Don't carry on like that."

Ann pinched Charles on the nose and then sat back in her seat. She slumped down comfortably and took another bite from her fruit. Charles was almost finished munching on his. Linda felt the jovial little show had subsided and returned to the almost finished brown barn.

Charles guided his car down the near-empty highway with his mind drifting on the things he and Ann had talked about. What was this world coming to? He pondered. The weather patterns had been so irregular lately, coupled with ozone alerts and high sulfur dioxide counts. Alcohol and drug rehabilitation programs were overloaded to the point of breakdown. Mental health institutions were overcrowded and many of Charles's own past acquaintances were now inmates of such institutions.

Charles rubbed his eyes and felt a gentle nudge while Ann handed him a paper cup filled with lemonade. Charles thankfully took the cup and rolled down his window a little more. The smooth-running car steadily piled up the miles toward their destination. Ann spotted a distance information sign along the side of the road.

"Hooray, alright! Ten more miles to Desert Springs. We just might make it yet."

Ann pushed the steering wheel horn in joyful glee, shocking Charles, who brushed her hand in jest.

"You're going to get us killed out here."

"Oh, Charles, you're so self-conscious. There's hardly anybody out there. What could we hit? A cactus?" Ann giggled after her comment. Charles reacted by gingerly frisking her hair.

Ann continued to tease Charles for amusement. Linda responded by kneeling up in the seat behind her mother. She gently put her arms around Ann, moving her hands up to Ann's mouth, indicating that she sided with her father.

"Majority rule," he said, winking at Linda.

In a few minutes, Charles angled into the blacktop driveway of the scenic resort. Standing three stories high was a beautiful red brick building surrounded by huge shade trees shadowing the handily manicured grounds. This contour was offset by precision lined finely cut shrubbery and a very unique cactus intermixed with rocks flowerbed near the entrance. Charles parked the car, got out and stretched by the door. Ann got out and stepped up onto the curb.

"I told Linda to stay in the car while we registered. The parking lot is so empty. Maybe they're closed," Ann said.

Charles walked around the car to Ann's side. Once adjoined they proceeded toward the entrance.

"There certainly aren't many cars out here," Charles remarked. "Maybe they have a lot of reservations for Saturday morning."

"Possibly," Ann replied.

When they reached the hotel's canopied entrance walk, an anxious bell boy greeted them enthusiastically. He then followed them to the front desk. A middle-aged youthful-looking desk clerk welcomed them with a broad smile.

"Thank goodness," the clerk sighed. "Am I glad to see some travelers? The business has been so bad the last few weeks." *I thought we were about to close down.*

He peered down into the guest book, turning to a near-empty page. "You should be Kellys. Am I right?"

Charles nodded confirmation while his eyes wandered around the plush lively-painted lobby.

"You can have your pick. Any room on the second floor."

"Why thank you, mister?" Ann focused in quickly and caught the clerk's name tag, "Hayes."

"Hayes, Hayes," Charles snapped his fingers trying to recall. "You were here last year, weren't you?"

"Yes," Mister Hayes commented. "Nice of you to remember."

"Oh, of course," Ann cut in now, "I remember. Does your wife still run the children's center during the day?"

"Yes, she does. That woman is quite a pusher. She helps keep everybody on their toes around here. I don't think the management appreciates her contributions. But I do. There's nothing like a good woman. Don't you agree, Mister Kellys?"

"You're dead right," Charles said with a wink.

Ann picked a center hall room that Charles paid for. He signed the guest book, placed the key in his pocket, and wished the clerk a good evening. Ann and Charles headed back toward the car to get Linda and unload the luggage. The bell boy courteously followed them closely to give assistance.

The room was a large bright beautiful one with double picture windows overlapping an Olympic-size swimming pool below. The bellhop drew the drapes and set the luggage inside, after which he stood waiting expectantly at the door for a tip. Charles pressed a five-dollar bill into the hand of the bellhop who left with his appreciation showing. Ann started unpacking the suitcases and putting things into the closet. Linda eyed the room over slowly. Charles sat on the bed and opened up the plastic bowl he'd taken from the canvas bag. It contained the fresh fruit salad Ann had prepared to stretch their vacation dollar.

"I'm fixing Linda a bowl of this," Charles said. "You want any?"

Ann nodded consent, so Charles set the three bowls on a table next to the bed. He dished up the three and took out a jar of orange juice from the cooler. Pouring three glasses, Charles handed Linda one and motioned Ann to have a seat beside him.

The meal was enough to send Linda off to a comfortable sleep. Charles and Ann watched television late into the night. They spent a romantic evening of fond remembrances in addition to planning Saturday's events.

A cool breeze that blew through the slightly opened windows assisted the Kellys's to a late morning sleep. Ann drifted groggily in and out of a semi-conscious state while Linda tugged on her arm. After seconds of incoherence, she rolled over and looked at the clock on the nightstand. Nine thirty-five. Ann slowly sat up in the bed, half-awake. A relieved |Linda embraced her with a warm hug. Charles opened his eyes and turned toward his family. He watched the pair in comfort close to each other. Charles thought about how lucky he was.

Linda signed to her mother that she was ready for breakfast.

"Don't worry, dear," Ann answered. "Right after we wash up, we'll go down to the dining room for the morning buffet."

When they passed the front desk on their way to the dining room, Charles greeted Mr. Hayes, who was seated reading a newspaper.

"Mr. Hayes. Good morning. How are you?"

"Very fine, Mr. Kellys. Did you sleep well?"

"Like a rock. Listen, Mr. Hayes, our friends, a Mr. Bill and Betty Roberts, were supposed to have arrived yesterday. Have they checked in yet?"

"No, I don't think so, but let me check."

Mr. Hayes pulled out his registration book. He was somewhat embarrassed at the few names listed during his fingered search of the pages. "Ah, I'm sorry. Mr. Kellys, but your friends are not here. Perhaps they'll be in later today."

"Thank you," Charles said before rejoining his waiting family.

"Are they here or has Bill canceled out?" Ann inquired.

Charles whimsically shrugged his shoulders, "No news may be good news."

The Kellys took their trays and helped themselves to the morning's selections. A friendly waitress brought anything else they wanted to their seats. Even at the special discount rates, the prices were expensive, but the food was excellent.

After breakfast, they strolled around the low grass-cut grounds in an effort to enjoy the natural surroundings. Charles sucked in air that somehow didn't seem so fresh, but the old adage of *country air is better than in the city* still applied. The greenery was beautiful, although a bit overworked. All in all, the grounds still had the aura of the great outdoors about it.

Halfway to the edge of the lawn area, Ann stopped and pondered intently for a moment.

"It's so quiet."

Charles stopped and listened carefully. "I don't hear anything."

"That's the point," Ann said. "There aren't any natural sounds. Can't you tell the difference."

Charles looked puzzled.

"No birds. Don't you remember those different kinds of birds that would land and nest around here? I don't hear anything now."

Charles shook his head as the oddity of the situation slowly dawned on him. "Yes, you're right. Those birds were all over this place. Come to think of it, I don't see any squirrels either, not any in the trees or running about the lawn. I don't see any signs of wildlife now that you mention it." As Ann reflected over the situation, Linda saw three other children playing by a sandbox on the resort's playgrounds. She began tugging enthusiastically on her mother's skirt while her other slender arm pointed at the three playing children. Ann's attention was broken from her pondering as she focused her attention on Linda.

"Oh, you want to go play with those children?"

Linda shook her head and pointed again.

"Do you think it's alright, Charles?"

"Sure," Charles answered, waving at a woman sitting on a bench not too far from the playing three.

"That's Mrs. Hayes. She's very good with children. She'll watch Linda."

Both parents waved as she ran off to play with the other three. Charles then turned toward his wife.

"Tennis, anyone?"

I thought you'd never ask.

Ann put her arm in Charles's waiting arm, and they headed for their hotel room to change attire.

The bright burning hot sun beamed down on them while Ann and Charles struggled through the twisting, exhausting running and chasing of balls all over the court. They both conceded that they were too out of shape for full-fledged games so they decided to pace themselves a little.

After an hour of missed serves and volleys that often landed over the fence, the couple sat down on a bench off to the side of the court. Sweating profusely, both gasped for air.

"This tennis stuff will kill you. I didn't know I was this out of shape," said Charles in the process of putting one foot up on the bench.

Ann was breathing so heavily she could hardly talk. She held one finger up trying to catch her breath to make a point. "If we played more regularly," she gasped, "we wouldn't have to make such fools of ourselves like we just did."

"Come on, Ann. We weren't that bad. Besides, there was nobody out here to watch us anyway."

"Well, I'm done for today," Ann stated, finally regaining some of her composure.

"Oh no, you aren't," Charles interjected playfully. "I'll race you to our room for swimwear. Let's take a shower and stretch out in the Jacuzzi. We'll totally forget everything for a few hours. Let some of those warm swirling vibrations massage our tired bones."

"Sounds good to me." Ann jumped up first. Charles found himself getting up off the ground after a mischievous push from Ann, who was already running toward the hotel.

"The last one there serves the pineapple juice!" Ann called out behind her.

Charles started sprinting, waving one finger in the air. "Wait! You cheated! No fair!" He chased Ann but to no avail. She won handily.

Upstairs, they drank some juice and dressed into the swimwear laid out on the bed after quick showers. Within a few minutes, the two were in the whirlpool. The warm water shot out of the whirlpool jet streams at the bottom of the tub. They both relaxed along the sidewall feeling the lavish comfort of the swirling water. Enjoying her husband's company, Ann started punching water at him which grew into a playful encounter.

Ann locked her arms around Charles's waist below the water surface, simultaneously putting her head on his shoulder.

"I can't get that strange silence out of my mind. Something is wrong, though I don't exactly know what."

"Don't worry, sweetheart," Charles reassured calmly. "I'm sure there's a logical reason for it. Maybe some new insecticide chased the birds away. I don't know. But we shouldn't worry about it."

"It's not only that," Ann countered, "this place is not the whole reason. It is how my heart feels. Somehow, I...I feel different. I can't explain it. I just feel strange."

Charles gave his wife a kiss, then looked into her dark brown eyes.

"Listen," he said gently but firmly, "we are here on vacation. Right?"

"Yes but—" Ann began.

"Ah, ah, ah," Charles cut in. "Let's enjoy ourselves. We don't know when for sure we'll be able to do this again. So, we better take advantage of it. We will worry enough about the world when we get back to it. Ann, let this weekend be ours."

Ann reluctantly agreed.

The two of them lounged in the whirlpool close to each other letting time drift by them. When they felt totally relaxed, Charles got out, leaving Ann.

"I think I'll go out for a splash in the pool."

"I'll join you, darling," Ann answered. "Give me a few more minutes here."

Charles went downstairs to the pool; Ann joined him about a half-hour later. From poolside chairs, they soaked up a little more of the sun which steadily moved.

Westward in the afternoon sky. Linda eventually joined them at the poolside, sipping on a festive-looking fruit drink.

As the day drew to a close, the Kellys got dressed and stepped over to the dining room for dinner. There were no diners waiting to be seated. In fact, there was only one other couple there. The Kellys sat across from Mr. and Mrs. Randolph Jenkins. They had flown in from Carson City, Nevada, earlier in the day. Mr. Jenkins was an older spry gentleman with a receding hairline and white hair. His wife was age lined and slightly puffy about the fact, but she had the appearance of someone with breeding. They were both overweight.

The two couples exchanged greetings along with small talk about general things.

"The surroundings here are quite unique," Louise Jenkins commented, "but I have never seen such a scarcity of vacationers at a hotel this size. Rather amazing when you think that this is the tourist season."

Ann and Charles agreed.

Mr. Jenkins cut in, "I still prefer this quiet little getaway over Las Vegas or Reno."

"We've been there so many times; I've still got slot machine bells ringing in my ears. This is our third trip here." The conversation sustained throughout their dinner. Mr. Jenkins owned a small exporting business, Perkins Coffee Imports Inc. He was up in years now and Mrs. Jenkins told Ann she had been trying to get her husband to retire from his responsibility-laden job for years, but it seemed he was a diehard workaholic.

This brought on a little old-fashioned sexist rivalry. Randolph defended his need to be away from home, engaged in meaningful activities. Charles agreed with Randolph.

They chatted about their particular family backgrounds. Jenkins had lived in Los Angeles. They left the overcrowded city when the youngest of their two children graduated from college. And now with the Jenkins brothers as business partners together overseas, Mrs. Jenkins felt it was the time that she and Randolph enjoy their golden years together.

Louise glanced over at Linda who was toying with some string beans on the side of her plate.

"Aww. A pretty little girl. All left out."

Linda signed to Louise that she didn't mind. To everybody's shock, Louise signed response in reply to Linda. Randolph looked momentarily surprised at his wife.

"My dear!" he exclaimed. "I didn't know you knew sign language."

"Why, I picked it up in the girl scouts," Louise said proudly.

"I'm not going to ask how long ago that was," Randolph joked as Ann and Charles chuckled at the remark.

Everyone rose up from the table in agreement to meet the next morning for breakfast.

They strolled across the way to the hotel, Linda and Louise in lively conversation.

"What a lovely girl you have, Mrs. Kellys," Louise said fondly, looking at Linda.

"Thank you," Ann returned. "We know she's special."

"Listen, I'm going down the road tomorrow after breakfast to an old antique shop. There are a few souvenirs I plan to pick up for friends. I would be very pleased if you would let Linda come along. Of course, if it is alright with Linda."

Linda shook her head and looked up at Ann.

"Sure," Ann replied warmly.

"I'm sure she'd be happy to go."

The couples waved goodnight in the lobby then proceeded to their rooms for the night.

The morning air had a snap to it as the Kellys stepped out of the dining room. Sunday morning breakfast had been delicious, and the same jovial party of the Kellys and the Jenkins strolled on the grounds in front of the hotel.

"I'm going to my room to grab a few things before we go to the antique shop," Louise informed.

"Okay," Ann answered. "Have a good time. Linda, behave yourself."

With Mrs. Jenkins's hand inside Linda's, they walked off toward the hotel while Ann and Charles continued on with Randolph on the hotel grounds.

He was a proud man full of vigor. Mr. Jenkins recollected dreams of owning a horse ranch when he was a youngster growing up in Kentucky. He talked about the hazards of getting established in business. His pace was somehow faster, and the pressures were greater. He didn't seem to like it so much as he was, by now, addicted to it. It seemed that the nature of becoming successful not only taxed a man of his dreams, but it made him more cynical about the world and the things around him. It seemed he'd lost touch with himself over the years. He no longer had any stirrings of the inner soul, of right and wrong, of God.

Mr. Jenkins was taken back by the recounts of his life. He talked of a time when he believed. Not just a shallow, every Sunday faith. But a deeply personal one. But that seemed so long ago. Back when things were simpler, less complicated. His faith was a great source of comfort to him. But as the demands of the world closed in on him, he had to make choices. One of them was to leave that quieter, more peaceful world behind.

Ann and Charles walked on either side of Randolph. They listened intently and with sympathy to his remembrances. Then, it all seemed at one moment, Ann and Charles got the same idea.

"Hey," Ann started as Charles perked up. "I got an idea, why don't you come down to the country church with us this morning?"

She put her arm in Randolph's and cast an inquiring glance at Charles.

"Splendid idea," Charles added. "It's just the thing for you. The services are usually very good even though we haven't been there in a while. It could be very inspirational. What do you say?"

Randolph looked at Ann, who was smiling cheerfully and brightly.

"How can I turn down such friendly people?" Randolph gave in. "I'll go with you."

"Great," Charles said with confidence. "The church is only a half-mile down the road and the service starts in half an hour. No need to get the car since we're all going. Let's just continue our leisurely little stroll on to the church."

"I'm with you." Ann threw in as the three of them headed down the road.

The church was a large wooden frame structure with stained glass windows and a point at the top that appeared to be a bell tower, although there was no bell in it. The Kellys and Mr. Jenkins stepped into the building and were quickly seated by the ushers.

"There seems to be a new pastor, according to this bulletin," Ann noted. Charles acknowledged her then turned his attention as the service was just beginning.

Following the church announcements, combined with the two stirring hymns by the young adult choir, the collection basket was passed. The Kellys and Mr. Jenkins contributed generously. A congregation prayer was next followed by a ten-minute devotional. At its completion, the baskets were passed down the rows of pew again, this time for the general offering. Once again, they gave freely.

A rather stocky and fairly young man listened as Pastor Fields took an upright stance behind the pulpit. He was very tastefully and expensively dressed.

"Life is beautiful. Love is beautiful. We all must try to fill this world with more love. We must give freely of ourselves. We must hold up our lights and let them shine on the world. The strong must bear the infirmities of the weak. He who has must extend himself. We must reach out to them who have not. Let the congregation say amen."

There were a few muffled 'Amens' in the house.

Randolph leaned over and whispered, "Looking at those expensive-looking rings and that diamond choker around his neck, I'd say he ain't doing too bad."

Charles diplomatically acknowledged the remark, but the tone of the whole event was beginning to worry him.

Halfway through the sermon, the collection basket circled the church for a stated needy cause. Ann and Charles contributed some change while Mr. Jenkins roughly pushed the basket on by him.

At the end of the message, Pastor Fields asked the congregation to contribute once more for the women's auxiliary fund. The Kellys refused to contribute again. While Mr. Jenkins, visibly disturbed by it all, backhanded the basket roughly, sending it tumbling to the floor. He then rose up fuming and stormed out of the church in anger. The Kellys excused themselves with the others in the church looking on with mild amusement.

Quickly leaving the building, Charles caught up to Mr. Jenkins, who was strongly pacing down the road back to the hotel, still fuming. Ann had to stride quickly to catch up.

Charles tried to explain that the church had changed since he'd last gone there. He offered that not all churches were that way, and he employed Randolph not to judge all ministers by the display he'd seen there.

Mr. Jenkins stopped and turned around, facing Charles. He shook his head in dismay and put his hand on his forehead as if trying to collect his thoughts.

"I know, Charles," he said with mustered calmness, "I'll try to keep an open mind. But it just doesn't seem like things will ever be the same. It's all just changed too much. The way people are today…I just don't know."

Charles put his arm around Randolph's shoulder and rubbed it gently as they both started up the road again. Ann caught up to his side.

"Randolph. I wish I could say the right thing. But I just don't know what to say."

They all walked back to the hotel in uneasy silence. When they got to the steps, they saw Louise and Linda sitting out front. Linda ran up to Ann showing the presents Louise had bought. She had a purse and two necklaces. Louise lugged a bag full of old knitting materials which Randolph immediately helped her with.

Ann thanked Louise for the gifts she bought Linda. Linda stood there smiling with delight.

Charles informed Jenkins that the family had planned an afternoon picnic in the nearby mountains. Therefore, they might not get a chance to see each other again due to an early morning departure. Both couples agreed on the enjoyment of the other's company. They exchanged addresses, phone numbers, and promises to stay in touch.

Genuine sorrow showed on Linda's face when she hugged the Jenkins farewell. Her parents gave their final goodbyes, and each party went to their rooms. The Kellys changed clothes, gathered the necessary equipment, ate lunch, and hit the winding road.

The aura of the mountains was so peaceful that the Kellys parked along a narrow pine bordered roadway at four thousand feet up. They got out for an intended short hike, but the family enjoyed the atmosphere so much they walked along the thick-brushed trails adjacent to the rock-filled ravines for hours, immersed in the fragrant scents. The picnic was completed in approximation to the sun's descension, signaling a chilling breeze.

When they returned to the hotel, they were exhausted. Ann and Charles hopped into the Jacuzzi donning their bathing suits so that Linda could join them. There they relaxed, letting the warm water massage them. Refreshed from the whirlpool, a late snack was all the Kellys needed to float into a comfortable slumber for the night.

Chapter 2
Coming To

The sky was gray, but not in a foreboding way, on this 1996 summer morning. Through the early morning fog, a silver Volkswagen Jetta cruised down Interstate 10, traveling west. Linda laid stretched out on the back seat. Charles and Ann were wide awake and alert as they watched the highway signs, passing coffee between themselves. Charles had been a little late getting started than he had planned, and thereby, he anticipated taking an unsavory route through town to save time. Monday morning was already off to a bad start.

The vacation, despite its unusual character, had been a success. Linda seemed to enjoy herself, and beneath all of the strange events, Ann and Charles still felt, somehow, well-rested. Their friends, the Roberts, however, never showed up; in fact, the resort remained, mysteriously, almost deserted the whole weekend. But Charles's desire to have a good time prevailed over the circumstances.

Linda tossed, yawned, and then sat up rubbing her eyes. Ann heard the movements and turned, looking back at Linda with a warm smile. When Ann turned back, she noticed in the distance, along the side of the road, an unusual figure that looked like a man. As the car grew closer, she recognized an old Indian dressed in full ceremonial attire.

"Linda, look at the Indian man." She pointed out calmly.

Suddenly, Ann felt an icy chill come over her. For just a flashing instant as the car passed, she felt as if her eyes had locked into contact with the Indian's.

Linda, smiling and mildly excited, pointed out the back window as the Indian faded in the distance.

"Charles," Ann began slightly shaken. "Did you see that Indian? For a minute I thought that…that he was staring at me."

"Of course. He saw the car," Charles replied.

"No, I don't mean the car," Ann countered. "He was staring at me. At me, you, Linda."

"I'd accuse you of being paranoid if so many other things hadn't happened this weekend. Actually, I wouldn't believe this whole trip if I hadn't been on it myself."

Ann kept pondering the incident solemnly as Charles, his mind fixed on making it to work on time, pressed the accelerator a little further in order to gain more time.

The green laced horizons and the rolling hills along the highway began to diminish as the Kellys entered the connecting chain of cities encircling Los Angeles. The traffic started to get heavier, and there were numerous motorcycles, mopeds, a few diesel trucks, and a variety of box-shaped compact cars in the commuter's convoy. Some drivers darted in and out and between others. Some were moving along slowly. Ann looked over and saw a short, stubby-looking man driving a loaded down station wagon. The huge bundles tied on the top of the car sagged it low to the ground with heft. He was driving with one arm resting his head, leaning out of a rolled-down window. Rock music was blasting from his radio. His car swerved from side to side in between the lane lines as he dozed and then caught himself.

"Now there's a real low rider," Ann joked as Charles caught a glimpse of the weighed-down station wagon. Charles laughed, pulling into the far lane carefully, avoiding the swerving wreck.

As they got closer to the city proper, the pollution became intense. The contrast of the thickening mist was most apparent after having been up in the cleaner mountain air.

Charles rubbed his eyes, which sensitively burned from the city atmosphere.

"Is it bothering your eyes again, dear?" Ann asked.

Charles was trying to clear some of the moisture; tears of irritation.

"A little bit. This stuff got worse last week when I made a run to cover the forest fires."

"Do you want some eye drops? I've got some in my purse. It's that new anti-sulfur compound. Special pollution formula."

"No, I'm alright," Charles responded.

"You know," he continued, "it's funny, the factories pollute the air, making products. Then, they turn around and make a product in a factory to help you get through the smog caused by them to begin with."

Ann looked puzzled for a moment as she tried to unscramble Charles's muse.

"The eye drops," Charles said, "to fight pollution. Why don't they just close down the polluting factories?"

Ann glanced over at Charles. "Oh, you know they can't do that. Too many people with money in Southern California, with the high cost of energy and transportation, the consumer goods must be nearby. So, the factories end up where the money is."

"Ahhh," Charles waved his hand. "Armchair economics. That greedy, money-clutching executives are gonna destroy the very air we breathe."

"Well, the governor says," Ann induced mockingly, "the oil shortage has reached crisis proportions. We have to use more coal, and that means more coal-burning factories."

"The governor also said he'd introduce better pollution control legislation."

"He did introduce a few new pieces, like the application of that Montgomery Method. I think it was artificial inversion or something like that." Ann thought about theft act for a moment. "I wonder why it never passed? The last anybody heard of it; some committees had it tied up in the house."

"Payola," came the lone sarcastic answer from Charles. "Special interest groups have so many lobbyists, they smother any good thing the legislature can bring up. Everybody's out for himself."

The Kellys reached their exit, Charles's shortcut, and turned off on a detour that was to take them partway through the inner city of Los Angeles. This was a part of the city they would have avoided were Charles not pressed for time.

Ann and Charles locked their doors as Charles maneuvered through the side streets, trying to get home quickly. He dashed down one street faster than the speed limit in an attempt to make the light at one corner when it changed on him, and he was forced to a screeching stop.

His car narrowly missed a huddled crowd of youths who were loitering near the light at the corner. He gripped the steering wheel tightly as adult men approached the car from the other side. One man exposed himself, laughing and pointing to Ann. The other two started pounding on the top of the car, demanding a ride and some money.

Charles pulled Ann close to him and shot an angered glare at the frantic men. Ann covered her eyes. The crowd of youths on the corner watched with amusement while a couple of women on the other side of the street laughed loudly and vulgarly. The tugging and rocking of the car, the cursing and demanding of the three hoodlums became so intense that Charles couldn't wait the three seconds or however long he had at the stoplight. He punched the accelerator and sped across the intersection, brushing off two of the intruders. He left the one who was holding onto the door handle rolling in the street. The vulgar women laughed even louder.

As the Kellys moved further down the boulevard, driving became more difficult with wanderers and vagrants lingering out in the street reluctantly or refusing to move. One elderly woman beckoned and even pleaded for Charles to roll over her as she knelt in obscenities at the car, while youths taunted the Kellys, some showing open, blind rage.

Many of the unemployed had given up the dream of peaceful coexistence because they felt unjustly denied the right to prosper; those who had personal convenience were viewed with contempt.

"The rich will pay!" one angry young man shouted, dressed in army fatigues and shaking his fist ferociously. Charles came to a stoplight that was not working at a busy intersection. He would not have stopped was it not for so many cars trying to get across at the corner. A large and somewhat organized-looking group, the younger members began beating on the back of the car and shaking it up and down by the bumper.

Linda grabbed her mother by the neck in terror. Ann screamed as she saw the leering faces of men and women lurking close to the door window.

Charles shouted, "Get out of my way! Let us through! I'm not rich. I'm just a working man."

Charles hit his horn and inched his way slowly forward while the frustrated crowd of the lost, the poor, the unemployed, and the forgotten pounded and demanded.

Charles closed his eyes momentarily and gritted his teeth tightly in utter amazement. No matter how bad he had imagined things to be; he had never thought that they had gotten this far out of hand. He inched his way far enough out into the intersection until the coming traffic had to stop. Others in the wild bunch of wanderers converged on other stopped motorists. Charles, viewing the opening once again, accelerated, leaving the rowdy group tumbling behind him. A man who was standing on the front bumper was thrown against the front end of the car across the hood and wound up on the pavement below.

Charles sped down the street, this time less concerned about the harm caused to the hoodlums harassing his family. He darted down an alley and made a couple of quick turns to pick up the interstate freeway again.

With the sweat of fear rolling down his face, Charles glanced at Linda, who was crying and clamped onto her mother. She had climbed into the front seat, almost jumping as her father had sped away from the hostile crowd. Ann was in near hysterics, clutching Charles's arm.

"Ann, you alright?" Charles shuddered while he wiped the tears with one hand from his daughter's face.

"My God, what is happening to this world? Those people are out of their minds. We are not the cause of the world's problems. They even broke the antenna off of my car."

Ann sobbed in remorse, "We are lucky, praise God, we are alive." She shook her head in bewildering dismay.

Linda kissed her mother on the cheek as she clasped Ann's hand tightly, consolingly. Linda's inner strength. Ann put her forehead next to Linda's and hugged her. Nothing else was said. They went over a bypass. Charles continued to stare unblinkingly at the road in front of him.

He wondered how much further things could go. He was pained and greatly disturbed for himself and more for his family. He felt an extreme bitterness inside. Strangely, however, his bitterness was not directed at the people who had just assaulted him. They were the poor, the disenfranchised, and the confused. They were powerless. It seemed that humanity was caught up in a tidal wave of confusion. People had become so caught up in themselves that they had no time for compassion. As the gap between the haves and the have nots widened, the mad scramble for the crumbs that were left became greater.

Drugs and perversion were running rampant at every level of society. The poor indulged to dull the hard facts of their reality. But for the well to do, it was a pleasure garden of earthly delights. And it seemed as times grew harder, more shortages, crises and further economic downturns. Instead of the populace drawing together to support each other, violent abuse was the norm of the times.

The Kellys left the highway on an exit a short ride up the way into a district that was more familiar to them. Their Pasadena neighborhood was unchanged. When they passed by a corner market and on their block, the tension they had felt before eased a bit. Linda, sitting in her mother's lap, felt relieved at the sight of the neighbor's homes. Charles and Ann had never felt happier to see their brownstone two stories before.

Chapter 3
Linda's Learning

The Volkswagen rolled to a stop in the driveway of the Kellys home. Charles turned the ignition key off in the midst of peculiar silence. The family sat for a few seconds in a sense of extreme relief, confusion, and sadness.

Linda looked out of the window at the front door, the threshold to her desperately needed security, and saw a sort of unusual festive air about it. Like little bright balloons welcoming them, she looked at the rose bushes around the front of the house in full bloom. It was an added welcome.

She smiled, pulled her mother's arm lightly, and pointed.

"Well, look at that," Ann said in a tone that shifted from sadness to surprise.

"What? Look at what?" Charles stated as if waking from some kind of daze?

"The rose bushes!" She got out the flowers in the cup of her hands. She marveled at the deep red petals. Charles came up behind her, holding Linda's hand.

Ann turned around and stated to Charles. "These bushes had totally dried up. They were all but dead two days ago. From nothing to full bloom. How could this be?" Ann was aghast.

Charles pressed his fingers into his eyes, massaging them, trying to comprehend what he saw. He raised his hand in thought up to his forehead and then gazed at the sky. There was a cloud formation in the shape of a cross that had been there for several days. At first, he paid little attention to it, but with the unusual incidents that were mounting; he mentally tried to hook the events together.

Ann followed Charles's skyward glance. "Oh, you've noticed it too," she said, standing up again. "It's been up there for several days. Do you think there could be any connection?"

"I don't know," Charles answered.

Linda, still holding Charles's hand, began slowly to nod her head. She pointed at the roses and then to the cloud formation.

Both Ann and Charles thought Linda's motions peculiar. They stood there in question for a moment. Then, Ann reached out and hugged her daughter, who came rushing longingly and lovingly into her arms. Charles kissed Ann, then he kissed Linda on the cheek and pulled out his keys to open the door.

Ann ushered Linda into the house while Charles went back to unload the car. The family was shaken and in wonder, somewhat slow and pondering in their movement; but the relentless day did not allow them to break a long established Monday morning pattern. Linda still had to be at school. Ann had a whole hospital depending on her head nurse duties, and as for Charles, of course; there was the news to get out.

Linda lay down on the couch, toying with the necklace Louise Jenkins had bought her.

Ann told her she could not rest now. She instructed Linda to go upstairs, wash up, and change clothes. Linda lethargically nodded understanding and soon went upstairs, obeying her mother's request.

Charles had unloaded the car and was upstairs putting his clothes out for the morning's work. When Ann came up, there was water running in the bathroom.

"Ann, what do you think happened to Bill and Betty? They told us they would meet us at the resort. I've known Bill since high school. He's not the kind to break his word."

"I don't know," Ann replied, pulling a pressed white nurse's uniform from the closet.

"Almost anything could have happened."

"Come to think of it, ever since Bill bought that twin-engine piper, he hasn't been able to stay out of the air. A couple of Saturdays ago, he told me he was getting so fed up with it 'I'm splitting' were the exact words, I bet they flew to the Cayman Island."

"For good?" Ann exclaimed.

"Maybe so."

Charles came out of the bathroom and began putting on his clothes, a gray suit with a blue shirt and dark tie. Ann went into the bathroom and after washing her face with cold cream soap, a task she found refreshing, she began applying rouge to her cheeks.

Ann Kellys had a beautiful face. She looked youthful yet very mature and responsible with a hint of playfulness in her eyes. Her brownish-red hair were cropped well and cut with precisely the right professional touch, and her delicate hands and slender long fingers fairly framed her features as she applied the rest of her make-up.

When Ann came back into the room, she found Charles already dressed and adjusting his tie. He was staring lovingly at a picture of Linda on the dresser.

"Linda had been adjusting to us very well. I had certain reservations when we first brought her home. She is being adopted…" Charles stammered for a moment, almost embarrassed, he then cleared his throat, "I mean cloned."

"Why do you still say 'adopted'?" Ann asked. "Things are changing. It's no longer looked down upon to have a cloned child. People don't think so bad of you if you choose to clone your child."

"Some people," Charles interrupted. "Besides, I love Linda, she's become such a part of my life that somehow, I just don't look at her as being a clone." Ann was pleased by the way Linda had helped him feel like a complete husband, a father. She had often noticed the special glow in his eyes when the public gave him that extra respect in a greeting. The type a family man receives. Charles and Ann had been married for thirteen years. They met at a New Year's Eve party fifteen years ago given by some of Ann's nursing school friends. When they had dated, Charles frequently talked about having children. He wanted children of his own. When Ann first suggested cloning, Charles was against it. The guilt he felt about his own sterility hampered his desire to go along with Ann. After much tenderness and understanding during long nights of conversation, Charles finally relented.

His reluctant agreement was not helped by the process which produced a child who was normal in appearance, but who lacked certain functional abilities. The institute worked with Linda for years allowing the Kellys to visit and bring gifts until she could function better in society.

When they brought Linda home, she still had special needs, but she was so full of vitality that the Kellys became instantly attached to her, their long-awaited child.

Charles stood up, looking at his watch. He paused, looking over at Ann, who was combing her hair in front of a wall mirror.

"Charles," Ann called out. "Open the bottom drawer and take out the photo album for me." Ann's remembrance struck a sentimental note inside of her. Suddenly, she had a longing feeling to reach back.

Charles hesitated while observing his wife's eyes; she seemed reflective, almost sullen. He then reached into the dresser drawer and pulled out a green bulky picture album, which he tossed on the large round bed.

"Don't you think we should start out?" he asked.

Ann put her comb on the nightstand and sat on the bed near the album. "Sit on the bed with me," she pleaded, "just for a minute."

Charles sensed his wife's need and sat beside her. She folded open the photo album which showcased their wedding pictures first. The gala event had been captured on film from every angle. Charles hadn't changed much over the years. He looked every inch of the six feet he was, standing shy and slightly nervous in his tuxedo. His dark hair and dark eyes were ever searching, always in awe like some little boy lost in the woods, yet amused by all the things around him. The pictures and shots of her and Charles together were arranged neatly over the next few pages.

Ann turned another page. She pointed to a photo of a stocky, amiable-looking young man.

"James Mitchell."

"Yes…yes," Charles answered. "He looks so frail these days. Stress and a bad marriage are doing him in. I warned him that Bianca was no good for him."

Ann went on to the following page.

"Look at little Linda, on the lawn in front of the institute in the cute yellow dress."

Charles acknowledged the photo and smiled warmly, "She acted more detached the longer she stayed at that place. But remember how she perked up and became full of life when she came home?"

Ann fumbled with a couple of pictures protruding from the plastic covering. "Home was what Linda needed."

"That old polaroid took such clear pictures. Whatever happened to the old thing?"

"Somebody stole it at work," Ann answered.

"Oh," Charles said, sounding almost disappointed. He closed the album and placed it behind them. "We'd better go."

"Slow down, tiger," Ann commented, reaching back and flipping the photo album open again. "We haven't come to my favorite part."

"Thought our wedding was," Charles shot back with a frown.

Ann turned to a middle page.

"It was special. But this is my most favorite."

On the page was a photograph of a slightly built pilot leaning against a tree, in Vietnam, draped in old air corps fatigues.

"Ouugh." Charles blushed and put his head in one hand, shaking it. "Nam was such a long time ago. Look at me."

"You looked like a stork in a flying suit," Ann joked.

They both laughed. Ann continued, "You looked like they were starving you to death, am I ever glad I learned how to cook." She pinched his ribs before he could stop her.

"Fatten up them old bones. Cooking was one thing my mom taught me and my sister."

"Dad, the old railroad man that he was, wouldn't look at a frozen TV dinner. He was a meat and potatoes man, and he always ate hardly. I wonder how they're doing now? I haven't heard from them in a while. Why don't we take a trip to Oklahoma and pay them a visit? They haven't seen Linda yet."

"Things are so expensive, Ann," Charles replied. "We'll see what we can do."

"There's old Willie Denard," Ann pointed, smiling.

"Yeah. He was our squadron leader. He had such a deep Georgian accent, we could barely make out what he was saying over the airwaves."

"Is he still married to that girl with the large nose? You know her name, it started with an S…" Ann paused to think.

"Sandra, Sandra Spielman," Charles replied.

"Oh yes, Sandra Spielman. Did she have an old schnozzola on her? It looked like a banana. I liked Sandra, but she was so funny."

"You can be cruel when you want to be. Ann, you know that's not nice," Charles jested. "You only stick up for her because she likes you."

"No, she didn't," Charles playfully defended.

"Yes, she did," Ann upheld. "I watched her at those parties when you were on leave."

"She used to stand in the corner making eyes at you."

"Ah, go on!" Charles waved his hand at Ann while he peeped down at another snapshot. "And there's Larry Hintz. He was shot down somewhere over Cambodia and was listed missing in action. Boy, what a waste! He was a top-notch pilot."

"Yes, you've talked about him before. I wish I could have met him."

"He was a good kid." Charles reflected a second or two, leaning backward. "You know, there's another reason to go to Oklahoma. I read in a Petroleum Industry research file last month that Larry's brother is a bit wheel in Tulsa. Come to think of it, they have an anchor spot opening up in our affiliate down there. I remember talking to him long-distance one weekend from Saigon. He seemed like a really nice guy. I told him we would meet again, and his connections could help."

"Well, then we should make it a date," Ann interjected.

"Easier said than done." Charles then closed the photo book for the final time. "Besides, I think we have dates with jogs that are far more pressing."

"You're right, dear." Ann leaned over and kissed Charles spontaneously on the lips. The passionate kiss sent a more deliberate rush through the couple, and a longer more passionate kiss followed.

Charles was leaning Ann back when Linda walked into the room needing her dress fastened, and her ribbons tied. Ann sat near the edge of the bed motioning for Linda to come close. She quickly fastened her dress.

"My leading ladies," Charles proudly commented.

He leaned forward and while holding Linda's slender shoulders, studied her eyes.

They were the happy, innocent carefree eyes of a child. But somehow, these eyes almost seemed like they were hiding meaning.

"Linda, if only you knew how much we really love you. How much you make this family complete."

Ann smiled as she tied the ribbons.

Charles stroked Linda's shining brown hair. A hint of regret came over his face, "If only you could talk."

Linda stood there smiling. Mute.

Ann then spun her around and hugged her gently. "But we love you with every bit of our love. We're your parents, and we're very proud of you. You're our sweet little girl and nothing will ever change that."

Charles felt slightly ashamed of his revealing moment of self-pity. He hid his feeling and changed the subject. "How are you doing in school. Have you got any new things to show your mom and me?"

Linda smiled, shook her head, and ran back to her bedroom. She returned a short time later with graded school papers. Charles looked at the marked papers intently before he handed them to Ann one by one.

"Very good," he commented while admiring large pieces of construction paper that contained an artwork. "This is excellent! Our little girl has talent. But of course. She has such a talented father."

"Ann modest too," Ann threw in.

"Time to go," Charles said sharply. He patted his knees after standing up and held his arms out for Linda. She readily hopped up, and he carried her downstairs with Ann right behind.

Ann went to the garage and backed out her sporty compact Chevy Spyder onto the driveway. She had gotten the car in celebration of her promotion four years ago. For a long time, she'd wanted a sports car, and though this was just an economy model; she was still very pleased with it. Linda ran out and climbed into the other front bucket seat. Charles leaned over and put his head in the window, kissing Ann quickly one last time.

"Don't forget to talk with Linda's teacher. Find out about that flashcard system she called us about last week. If it sounds good, we'll work with Linda on it. I'm fairly busy these days, but I'll make time."

"I'll see you two this evening."

He winked at Linda.

"Don't be too hard on the teacher."

Charles watched the pair drive down the tree-lined street. He checked the front door again and then climbed into the silver Volkswagen. The family had all but recovered from the harrowing events of the morning.

As he drove off their neighbors, the Richardsons were leaving their white two-story colonial. He was a middle-aged insurance broker, and his wife worked as a claim's adjuster for the same company.

"Such a lovely couple with good-paying jobs," he remarked. "I wonder why they grafted that little mute clone?"

Mrs. Richardson opened the car door. "I don't know. Maybe they couldn't have one of their own."

They both got in. "Well, everyone on the block has had something to say about it. I would tell Charles, but he is so sensitive about the thing…uh, it…uh, the child or whatever it is."

"Don't meddle, Avery," Mrs. Richardson retorted as Mr. Richardson reversed the sedan out of the driveway and on to work.

After a fifteen-minute drive, Ann and Linda pulled into the crowded parking lot of the United Handicapped School which was about three miles from their home. There were several orange vans unloading with the attendants assisting the crippled, deformed and handicapped youngsters. Some of the children seemed extremely anxious. The school was the high point of their lives. For at least eight hours during the school weeks, they didn't feel odd or unusual.

Some of the boys broke free and ran away playfully from the school aides. Some behaved like unbridled stallions freed after a long corralling. Two mute girls stood against the brick wall and gestured messages in Linda's direction. Ann asked Linda if they were her friends and got a widely nodded yes. The girls came over to Linda and grabbed both her hands, swinging her arms. They tried to entice Linda to skip with them, but Ann held Linda back. She wanted her presence when she talked to Mrs. Wilson, Linda's teacher.

They entered Linda's very decorative classroom and an attractive thin woman with graying hair in her early fifties stood and greeted Mrs. Kelly. Ann returned the greeting as the two exchanged pleasantries. Linda sat in a chair beside her mother.

"How is Linda coming along in class these days, Mrs. Wilson?"

"I can't give you a definite answer," Mrs. Wilson began, "she is a bright girl, normally very patient, but lately, she had been showing signs of listlessness. Her mind seems to be somewhere else. Are there any problems at home that might be causing this?"

Ann thought for a moment, "No, nothing I can think of. She behaves basically the same way she always has. Although I've noticed she does seem to take her prayer times more seriously. Sometimes, it is almost like she sees something. Something Charles and I don't, but I can't call that so unusual. Maybe a few of us parents could stand to be a little bit more devoted to meditation."

Mrs. Wilson gave no reaction whatsoever to Ann's statement. She glanced again at Linda who was examining the plants lined along the window ledge. The teacher then reverted back to Ann.

"I have some important learning aids for you." She walked over to a large box of flashcards.

"It's the Montessori Special Education plan for the speech-impaired children. This deck of flashcards has a grouping of pictures, letters, and word identification. This material is specifically designed to challenge the youngster in a fun way. The attention span of a hyperactive child should increase if the parents are willing to give the time. Now, I know that Linda is not hyperactive per say, but I thought it would help if the parents worked with the teachers here at school. Perhaps the extra effort will bring Linda out of this preoccupied state."

"I'm sure it is merely a phase," Ann commented.

"You're probably right, Mrs. Kelly, but we must give all the understanding we can in a situation like this. Linda should always know that there is something caring close around."

Ann took the box of cards from Mrs. Wilson and placed them in her purse.

Active children began to enter the classroom. Many of them talked about, poked at, and made fun of each other. Mrs. Wilson immediately clapped her hands loudly and stomped on the floor until she got everyone's attention. The students were soon quiet.

Ann thanked Mrs. Wilson for her concern and time. The teacher was gracious. Linda waved goodbye to Ann as she left the room. Ann walked down the hallway and through.

Chapter 4
Charles' Dilemma

The double doors at the entrance reassured that the extra expense they were paying for the special education was money well spent. She soon made it to her car and was en route to the Los Angeles Medical Center.

As Charles drove to work along the freeway, he looked up into the sky and kept focusing on the image of a cross that had formed in the clouds. The image was directly in front of him as he entered the city limits of Burbank. This strange image and the peculiar events that were adding up definitely had some unified meaning. But just what it might be? He was puzzled.

In time, Charles drove up the long winding driveway in front of the KGBH TV station. It was part of an entertainment complex that included several movies and TV production facilities and back lots. His department was housed in a four-story concrete structure protruding toward the front of the complex. A large cast stainless steel sign marked the station in bold letters. When he pulled up, there were a couple of dozen protestors, some hippie types, other very conservative-looking with picket signs, marching along the narrow sidewalk.

"We want action!" one of the protestors demanded as they saw Charles Kelly's car slow to a stop.

"Liar! Liar! You're all a bunch of liars. You're nothing but pig lackeys for the establishment rich!" the protestor, young, handsome, and very aggressive, directed these comments at Charles as he climbed out of his car.

Charles gave no response but maneuvered his way through the protestors and up to the front door.

"Pig! Pig!" a protestor began to shout when he saw no reaction from Charles. He then began chanting as the other protestor joined in.

"Liar! Liar! Tell the truth! Liar! Liar! Tell the truth."

The group of protestors broke into a frenzy as the valet clad in a black turtleneck and sports coat with a Greek cabbie hat passed Charles, greeting him, coming for the car keys. The muscular young man seemed totally unaffected by all the protesting only a few feet away from him.

"Mr. Kellys. Good morning. How was your vacation?" he inquired, more out of courtesy than interest.

"Oh, it was nothing spectacular, but we did manage a decent time," Charles handed him the keys. "Warren is in my space so park it on the far end."

The valet nodded at the instructions.

Then, in a more confidential tone, Charles leaned over and spoke directly to the valet. The tall valet focused downward while he absorbed Charles's inquiry.

"What are they demonstrating about this time?"

"Ah, from what I can gather, they're protesting for a truer version of the news."

"They say, there are too many nice-nice features, too much cheesecake, not enough substance. It seems the last straw was that advertised new segment by Linda…whatever her name is. Uh…animal stories or something like that."

Charles looked down and shook his head in regret. He muttered to himself, "I told that blow-hard Rogers not to run that piece!"

"If you ask me," the valet added, "for the first time, I think I'd agree with them."

Charles came into the lobby and signed in with a security guard who was visibly nervous and on edge. He took the elevator up to the third floor and entered what up to now had become an all too familiar sight. Electric typewriters were clicking, and phones were ringing as impatient reporters, researchers, and secretaries busily answered, discussed, and haggled over a copy. There were white-coated technicians buzzing around dozens of electronic terminals and copy feed analyzers along with the sophisticated word processors. Huge black cables lined the floors running off of these electronic monsters.

Charles walked to his desk and set his briefcase off to one side. He looked over the mail and memos piled on his desk. The reporters and secretaries were friendly and cordial as they walked by. Some joked with him about his vacation while others chided him about putting on a couple of pounds. Bah! Charles rebuffed. They were seeing things.

No matter how he tried to get into his workday and pick up on his assignments, Charles Kellys could not get it out of his mind that the news director, Bernard Raymond Rogers, had disregarded his advice and run the P.R piece: Linda Colvin's Animal Stories. There was already too much sidetracking, feature stories, and personality pieces in the six o'clock news as it was. The happy news format with the disk jockey style anchor persons was, he thought, compromise enough. He thought the taste pieces on nude dancing at fine restaurants, not to mention sex in the street, displaying full nudity, was ridiculous but to add even one more mushy segment to an already sap laden hour of news was the final straw! What was Rogers trying to do? Cover up the hard news with this half-baked stuff?

Charles, annoyance building within him, got up and went over to the teletype. The wire service was busy, rapidly burning in through laser screen the latest news from all around the world. Charles picked up the end of the yellow folds of paper that were steadily rolling out a little at a time down to the floor.

Earthquake in Western Chile…113 known dead. Military over in Peru. The seventh military coup in the last six months. Archbishop: Sao Paulo, Brazil assassinated.

Putting his head down, Charles gritted his teeth. His mild annoyance was turning to anger. He shifted up a few pages…Pretoria, South Africa: Black workers riot. 16 killed; 37 wounded when combat soldiers shot into protesting crowd. Drought in East Africa, death toll mounts. Red Cross is sending relief to drought-stricken areas.

He turned and called for a copy boy who was headed for the city editor, Melvin LeClair's office.

"Randy," Charles called out impatiently, "let me see a copy of the early morning edition."

The copy boy, pencil behind his ear, shuffled through some papers in his hand as he detoured his over to Charles who was waiting expectantly by the teletype. He handed Charles a stack of papers, which Charles snatched and began to read through with a great degree of irritation.

"What is this?" he demanded. He began to pound the pages one by one on a nearby desk.

"Crop reports!"

He pounded another page, "Summer fashion?"

He then stood there, holding pages in both hands, raising his arms in dismay, speaking as if to the ceiling.

"Sid Nero, Rock star. Having her third child? What kind of news is this? There is hardly any hard stuff here. What are we? Some kind of social calendar?"

Charles slammed the papers on the desk amidst the stares and hushed tones of the startled wondering staff.

He immediately walked out of the newsroom and down the glass-lined hallway until he came to the Rogers's office. Knocking hard and firm twice, he twisted the knob and bolted in. The news director, who was quite an experienced newsman, calmly and nonchalantly motioned for Charles to sit down.

Charles stood and leaned over the director's desk. He was in no mood for cordiality.

"Have you seen this morning rushes?" Charles demanded.

"Seen them?" Rogers enquired almost whimsically. "I okayed them. What are you talking about, Kelly? You know nothing goes out of here without passing my desk."

"It's all title and irrelevant nonsense! What are we running around here? Is this a news bureau, or isn't it?"

"Exactly, what's on your mind, Charles?" Bernard Rogers focused in, in a more serious tone.

"It's the news," came the direct answer from Charles. "Or the so-called news."

"Lately, our editions are becoming shallower. We've been sticking in too many soft features. What are we trying to do? We can't soft-sell the people. It's in the public's interest to be informed."

"Don't read the reporter's rules of the road to me, Kelly. I was putting out the news when you were too young to even know what it was. Sure, it is great to have that purest attitude. But the bottom-line, boy, is ratings. We, here at Channel 2, have been the number one news station for eight years running. We didn't get that way from reading doom and gloom for sixty minutes! We reached this peak by giving people what they want!"

"I know that," Charles cut in, "and I accepted that long ago, but lately, I think we've been getting too imbalanced."

"Imbalanced!" Rogers became visibly upset. "Don't tell me how to run a station, boy! I've got all kinds of considerations and pressures over my head. You see that chart over there?"

Charles looked over to a wall loaded with plaques and awards and followed Mr. Rogers's finger to a multi-colored graph showing the rating to date.

"Channel 13 has been catching us in the ratings, ever since they hired that balloon bosomed weather girl to bump and grind her way through the daily forecast. How do we compete with that?"

"I'm sure rating is important, Mr. Rogers, but I think we have some kind of moral obligation to our audience. We can't just show all soft stuff. The news is for information."

"Moral obligation…Ha! That's you all the way, Kellys. You sit in your Sunday Church services and wear your religion on your sleeve like you're some kind of a saint, moralizing to everybody. Well, come back down to earth!

Ratings aren't only important. They are everything! If we didn't keep those numbers up, we would all be out of a job."

Charles's resistance began to break. He saw he was getting nowhere. He changed his demeanor and began to speak more softly.

"All things aside, what about me, Raymond? What about our friendship and your relationship with my family? Doesn't that mean anything to you? Why didn't you take my advice about that animal story thing? I was requesting it with what I thought was sound judgment?"

"Listen, Charles, sit down." Raymond Rogers poured himself another cup of coffee.

"I loved your father. General Kellys was as fine a man as I have known. I've been a friend of the family since, well, before you were born. But matters are different. I have over a hundred and twenty people under me. Depending on me. I tell you that Channel 13 is doing anything and everything to catch us in the ratings. I'm getting heat from upstairs.

"Look, Charles. I didn't want that animal segment any more than you did. But we had to do something to counter that flossy weather girl at 13. You understand my situation, don't you, Charles? These things are decided by circumstances. It is out of our hands. It's out of control.

"I'm an old newsman, Charles. I worked for the St. Louis Post-Gazette, The Times, The Journal, heck! You name the job, I've worked it. I don't like this mis-mash any more than you, but it is the hard reality of our times. You understand that, don't you, Charles?"

Charles shook his head and looked around the room uncomfortably. He shifted in his chair, then came his reluctant answer.

"Frankly, no."

His statement then became firmer, "No, I don't understand. I don't understand how a news bureau with this caliber of workers and this amount of resources behind it can continue to go along with, this...charade! How can twelve wire services and sixty locals in the field produce such mindless dribble? NO! This, I do not understand."

The new director's patience had run out.

"I'm doing my job! And your job is to go get the news: where I tell you to do, and when I tell you to go. KGBH is number one, and it's going to stay on top! I don't care what I have to do...or who I have to fire!"

Rogers hesitated and stared directly into Charles's eyes deliberately, "This department will tell the public what the public wants to hear. This viewing pays our bills, not the other way around. You got that, Kelly?"

The news director caught the change of expression which only made him angrier.

"To you, I've sold out. Is that it? Am I reading your thoughts right, mister hotshot Christian? You people kill me. You go around moralizing to everybody, spouting off your high falootin' purist attitudes! You go to your church and think the only people worthy of anything are between those stained-glass windows. Open your eyes, wake up man! Everybody doesn't have the same feelings. Moral obligations…that's a joke. Do goody stuff may work fine on paper, but it doesn't mean a hill of beans out here.

"I'm a businessman. Everybody's out there getting theirs, and I'm getting mine. Every person doesn't have time to consider moral obligations. Do you think if any of those poor slobs out there asked for ten million dollars or ten dollars for that matter; it would fall out of the sky? No. Of course not! They have got to get it in the streets and work for it. I've been working for over twenty-five years in the news business. From my work, I've earned money and respect. I'm an admired man. The public listens to me. People all over town trust me, my editorials, my opinions, my judgments.

"Charles, I deal with all kinds of people every day, big shots, revolutionaries, newsmen, critics. I take heat from all sides of the desk, and you won't have the comfort of seeing life through rose-colored glasses. I'm not just telling you this for my health. It is high time you learn how to handle people, the way I'm handling them.

"You've been a good reporter, Kelly. We need men like you on this staff. But take your God and your moralizing and deal with it on Sunday. Leave the rest of the world to itself."

Charles was beyond the point where he cared to listen anymore. It was like talking to the wind or to the four walls. Bernard Raymond Rogers was like a stone. He turned when he perceived Mr. Rogers to be thorough and walked toward the door. His boss felt a little nervous in the stomach after all the tension of the argument. He rubbed his abdomen, shook his head, and picked up the mornings copy of the Wall Street Journal as he leaned back in his swivel chair.

Charles walked down the hallway with an angered, bewildered look on his face. A few of his co-workers who passed him motioned to speak but thought better of it after catching his scowl. As he walked briskly toward the elevators, Kurt Lindaquist, a friend and associate, called out from behind.

"Hey, Charles."

Charles Kellys didn't immediately respond.

"Charles. Hey man, slow. What's the matter?"

Charles turned at the elevator. He was trying to change how he felt to give Kurt a civil reception, but he was failing miserably.

"Nothing. Nothing at all, Kurt. Uh. Look I don't want to talk about it right now, alright? I'll talk to you later."

The elevator doors opened and Charles stepped inside. Kurt puzzled while the doors slowly closed, separating him and his friend. He tilted his head in question. He then straightened his tie and leisurely walked down to Bernard Raymond Roger's office. Upon entering the room, he found the new director dropping Alka seltzers into a glass and puffing on a big smoking cigar.

At the Medical Center, Ann Kellys was going over some of the reproduced charts placed on her desk for the seventh ward. She was at the ninth-floor nurses' station, the doctor's rounds were over, and it was break time. It had been a hectic morning with three patients on that floor alone passing away. Their beds were filled quickly by more influential patients on waiting lists, either at their homes or from some other more crowded hospital. Some of the less fortunate patients, without any influence, who lined the corridors in wheeled beds, had been particularly demanding today. One had grabbed hold to Ann's arm and had to be pried loose by two orderlies.

Ann sat making mental notes. She thought about Linda and the flashcard system she'd received this morning. Linda didn't seem as restless as her teacher said, but she was a special child, and she needed special attention. Nurse Kellys sat with her elbows on the desk with her chin resting in her folded hands. All was relatively quiet for the moment, and Ann wanted to be part of the tranquility. She was visibly disturbed, however, by loud gum popping as she turned around and saw Louise Hubbard, the ward secretary. She was smacking and twisting the gum with her middle finger in and out of her mouth while she read a Hollywood secrets magazine. The young lady was attractive, but she wore too much make-up, and her deep red lipstick looked as if it had been applied with a paint roller.

The phone began to ring at the desk, and Ann looked over at the secretary. She didn't budge.

"Would you get that?" Ann asked politely.

"I'm on break," came back the snappy answer from the secretary who only momentarily looked up from the magazine.

Ann glared at Louise, who apparently couldn't have cared less. She then picked up the phone herself.

"Hello? Dr. Griswold? One moment please, I'll page him for you."

Ann swung around in the chair and clamped a lever down on a microphone setting directly to her right.

"Dr. Griswold, Dr. Griswold. I have a Gloria Greenspan on line seven."

Shortly thereafter, a squat aging doctor came stepping down the hallway with a file under his arm. He had a proud arrogant glide and the cut-off spectacles that he wore sat prominently on the edge of his nose.

"I'll take it from here, nurse," he picked up the phone and began speaking.

Two young nurses who were at the water cooler leered at the doctor who was married but had a reputation for indulging in extra-marital affairs. Ann stood patiently by the doctor, collecting her thoughts for she had been meaning to talk to the busy, work laden neurosurgeon about Linda.

The doctor cast a haughty glance at Ann who he perceived to be listening in on his conversation. She was not. He turned his back, however, covering the phone a little more and spoke more softly.

As he finished his conversation and hung up the phone, he nearly ran over Ann hurriedly trying to get to the patient files.

"Get out of my way, nurse!" he shouted as he walked around her and slid the file drawer open.

Doctors were no longer registered at the hospital but were assigned by the AMA. They were an elite group among society and only came into the hospitals to look after cases the nurses and paramedics couldn't handle. They were also responsible for any surgery done. Doctors had attained such a high pay scale combined with such tremendous autonomy that they had become a caste unto themselves. The majority neither knew nor cared to know most of the hospital staff and many of them could be found hobnobbing on the beaches and golf courses with the most prestigious politicians and Hollywood stars. It always seemed like they were forever in a hurry, not because they let their caseloads back upon them. Partly result of the stringent social life.

Ann was hesitant and nervous, but she knew she had to seize upon this opportunity. Most doctors she had seen didn't have time for small talk. Physicians didn't want to be bothered with people's problems were they not related to something they were already involved in; and this doctor was a specialist. If a general practitioner was lofty, a specialist was all the more so. She knew all these things, but she had to take a chance.

"Uh, doctor," she began, still not having her words organized.

The doctor turned around irritated, shuffling through a stack of files he'd just pulled out. "Yes…yes…what is it?"

The doctor cut in. "Come, come, girl, I haven't got all day. What is it?"

"My daughter…my little girl," Ann motioned with an almost pleading tone in her voice. "She…she's got a problem."

"Get on with it," the doctor cried impatiently. "I've got work to do. What is the problem?"

"My little girl," Ann began again, this time speaking quickly under the fear that he might walk away at any moment. "She has a problem. One that was with her from the beginning…since the first day we had her."

The doctor lowered his glasses and raised one eyebrow. "What do you mean since the first day we had her?"

"Uhh," Ann whispered anticipating the reaction she knew she'd get from him, "she was cloned. On my husband's side." She caught the condescending look from the physician but pressed on.

"She's a mute, doctor. Totally unable to speak. I was thinking, with all the advances they've made in these areas that I could set up some sort of arrangement with you. Or maybe you could suggest someone. I need the information. About procedures, relative costs, which way is the best to go, which methods are the most effective for cloned children? I'd appreciate any information you could give me."

Dr. Griswold was standing there irritated with a smirk on his face, looking over one of the files he had singled out. Ann wasn't even sure he had listened entirely. He kept three files and placed the others back into the file drawer, slamming it shut.

The nurses in the background who were concluding their breaks reveled in the scene that was taking place. They actually seemed to enjoy the arrogance of the doctors. It somehow added to their sex appeal.

"Well, I'm the king of pressed for time, nurse," the doctor said disinterestedly. "If you'll make an appointment with my secretary, maybe I'll get back to you," he smiled blankly. "Have a nice day, miss." He then turned and unsympathetically pleaded, "I'm a busy man, nurse. You understand?"

As he walked down the hallway, Ann felt a little empty inside. It wasn't only the cold shoulder she had gotten from Dr. Griswold, it was the whole system. Physicians seemed to love the sense of power they held in their hands. The feeling of absoluteness. The power of life and death. She thought, sometimes the doctors behaved as if they were God.

She shook her head and smiled to herself at the thought. How absurd. A bunch of mortals, playing God. Could they not see their own limitations? With all the new technological advancements and all the electronic equipment, there were still points beyond which no doctor could go. When it was time for a person's brain to die, no one could keep it alive. A limp body could lie there being artificially nourished and organs being continuously respirated. But when the brain was gone, the body was merely a lifeless shell. No, doctors were not God.

Ann sat down again. She was undaunted by the doctor's disinterest. She'd find a way. She began surveying the photocopied charts once again.

Charles Kellys sat with his back to the wall in one corner of the television station's cafeteria. His bout with the news director left him without desire for the company for the moment. He could see everyone from the position he sat in. Thus, he could avoid contact with anyone he didn't care to talk with. He'd lift the newspaper higher in front of his face.

His ploy did not deflect Kurt Lindaquist. Kurt saw through it. He ambled over to Charles with his tall six-foot-four frame and sat across from Charles at the small round table and leaned forward.

"Rogers had been trying to page you. He wanted to talk to you. To apologize. He asked me to help find you. I knew where you'd be."

Kurt then intoned Charles on behalf of Raymond Rogers, "Come on, Charles. Why don't you go back up there? Let him talk to you. I don't know what he told you, but he seemed kind of upset about it. Give him a chance. He doesn't apologize often."

"I can't believe that guy up there," Charles said solemnly, "with all the calamities going on. It's as if somebody let the cat out of the bag. People are going crazy. All kinds of droughts and famines. The weather is going haywire. Heck…you can't tell the seasons apart anymore. The world is getting ready to blow up all around us. An what does he want to run? Animal stories!"

"Come on, Charles. You know how Rogers is. He's got a lot of pressure on him. He likes to keep a tight ship. It keeps his head clear." Kurt folded his hands and pressed them tightly while he made a point.

"Me and you, we're just a couple of crack reporters. We don't need to get involved in that programming stuff. We'll both be better off if we keep our mouths shut and pick up our pay checks. Look around man, we've got things pretty good."

Charles rose up and looked at Kurt like he had instantly gotten an idea. "That's it! That's what's wrong with things now. Going along. Picking up our checks. Smiling, bending over to please the next guy, cover your rear end. That's exactly the problem."

"Well, Kurt. Someday, somebody is going to have to stand up. To stick their neck out. There are political, economic, and social problems pressing all the major industrialized nations of the world. The world is getting ready to blow up in our faces. And what do we do? What do we, who can do something about it, do? We sit on our hands."

"You can't rock the boat, Charles," Kurt tried to answer Charles's question pragmatically, "especially if you're in it. You run the risk of tipping the whole thing over. You have to look out for yourself."

"I know I have to look out for myself," Charles replied firmly, "but at whose expense? Can I justify living in the clouds when everyone else lives in a mud hole? Sure, I'm a privileged person. I have access to all kinds of information the average man can't reach. But does that mean then I should simply forget about the people who are not so privileged?

"Look at us, Kurt. We joined the staff at about the same time. Two wide-eyed cub reporters who wanted to uncover and expose the problems of the world. Remember when the word 'scoop' meant something? Look at us, Kurt, look at what has happened to this whole blasted division. We're running around like little moles covering our rear ends. Going on assignments when we don't even know whether they'll ever be used or not. When this station back shelves or covers up an important story, we're as much to blame as the management. We are culprits too because we stood by and did nothing. The public puts their trust in us to inform them, and we let them down. What's happened? What has happened to us, Kurt?"

Kurt stared at his hands folded on the table. Charles's remembrances of their cub reporter days, in contrast to the soft arguments he had just raised, made him feel almost foolish.

"I don't know, Charles."

Charles thought about the burst of statements; he'd made. He saw the somewhat hurt look on Kurt's face, "I'm sorry friend, I didn't mean to take it out on you. I know it's not your fault."

He looked at Kurt and flashed a dim smile. "Hey! Is that dinner date still on with the family for tonight?"

Kurt nodded but didn't smile back. "Yeah, it's still on. The wife and I were kind of looking forward to it."

"Well, great." Charles stood up. He cleared his chair as Kurt rose, and both of them walked out of the cafeteria into the lobby. The number of protestors had increased drastically and shouts from could be heard all around the building. Kurt and Charles watched the angry mob through the plate glass windows while security guards scuffed with the demonstrators. When they turned and headed for the elevator, a large crashing sound pierced the air. Glass started flying around them as pieces slid across the floor beneath them. They hit the floor and turned to see a brick laying amidst the debris.

"Liars! Liars! Shut them down!" shouted one protestor. "Kill the rich pigs who bury the truth! Liar! Diseases! Earthquake! Will we all have to die before we learn the truth? Liars! Pigs!"

The protestor was felled by one crack of a security guard's swinging baton. Charles lay on the floor, thinking that for all of the violence, in fact, the protestor was closer to the truth.

They both got up off the floor.

"You alright?" Kurt asked.

"Cut my finger," Charles replied, "nothing serious."

The elevator came and the two boarded it and went up to the third floor.

Charles knocked on Mr. Rogers's office door, this time a bit less tense. He walked in, and Mr. Rogers actually seemed surprised to see him.

"Charles, sit down, have a seat." He offered Charles a cigar.

"Oh, that is right. You don't smoke." Mr. Rogers propped himself back in his chair and got comfortable. "Listen, Kelly, I'm going to be square with you. I only hired that girl till the end of the year. A little insurance you see. When we're satisfied with our numbers, we'll put her on assignment, and this animal thing will be over and done with. I'm also pressing the boys upstairs for a new five-minute segment dealing with the arms race, you know. Real hard gusty stuff. It's going to be touch and go but with right maneuvering, we could have something out by the middle of next year."

Charles sat motionlessly. He appreciated what Rogers was trying to say, but he had no reaction.

"Well?"

The news director swept the air with his hand, holding the large cigar in it.

"I don't know," Charles blankly answered, "what do you want me to say?"

"Don't you think it's a good idea?" Rogers sounded almost disappointed.

"The idea itself is good," Charles began, "but if you want my real opinion, your idea is like putting a band-aid on cancer. This whole thing didn't begin with animal stories. It's been a long slow process that has eventually compromised the professional character of every true newsman and woman at this station. It is cancer, Raymond. It's eating the heart out of the whole organization." Bernard Raymond Rogers's eyes began to bulge. Charles was not only unaccepting of the apology; he was almost insulting.

"You still don't get it, do you, Kelly? You can afford to walk around here on a cloud with the world in your pocket. Don't you think I see what's going on out there? The catastrophes, the famine, the disease, the misery? Don't you think I see that? Incidents are happening every day that would have been front-page stories-of-the-year in my day."

"Look at this." Charles leaned over and glanced at stack of papers marked confidential. They were news items. Strange items, the information he'd never heard about or seen before. Rogers forced the stack of papers in his hands.

"I gleaned these off of last week's wire service confidential."

Charles looked confused.

"Wire service confidential? I never even heard of that."

"And you won't." Raymond Rogers shot back. "Not until you get a little higher up in the organization."

"Look at that top story for example. On the top of the stack."

Charles read quickly and quietly to himself. It stated that two workers at Westwood Diagnostics were contaminated by an artificially produced virus that was intended for a new malaria vaccine. This man-made virus was of higher contagious perspiration and fever, followed by extreme paranoia and delusions, and eventual death. Authorities were following leads but had no idea as to the whereabouts of the two.

Charles looked up and suddenly felt a rush of the blood of his head. He felt the chill run through his body at the very thought of it.

Mr. Rogers saw the extreme reaction to merely the top story and snatched the stack of papers back from him.

"Tell me I don't know what's going on, Kelly!" Roger demanded almost mockingly. "We get news in here that you never even see. You talk about being a purist, moral obligations, about hard news! This is hard news, Kelly!"

Charles stood in a state of confusion. He was trying to read between the lines. Trying to sort out in his mind what Raymond Rogers was driving at.

"Shouldn't we alert the public about this?" Charles stammered. The question seemed so elementary. Almost mindless, compared to the implications of the potential epidemic.

"And what then?" came Roger's answer. "Cause such a city-wide panic that the National Guard would have to be called out. More people would be killed in the confusion than those two guys could infect in a week. We're playing against time."

"The stacks of stories? What about them? Are they all that serious?"

"Some of them are some are worse."

The impact on Charles was overwhelming. Here it was, a news bureau hired and paid to put out the news, a constitutional right, involved in a blanket across the board conspiracy to cover it up. The thought was shattering.

"I can't believe it," Charles choked. "You mean, yourself and those in upper management make life and death decisions like this in our board meetings?"

"I've already told you too much, Kelly. I can't say any more."

Charles looked at Rogers in total disbelief. "Who do you think you are? You can't sit in some meetings like the high council and make grand proclamations like that! These are human beings you're talking about. You can't play hide and seek with people's lives!"

There was a long pause and a moment of silence. Bernard Rogers leaned back in his chair. A saddened, disarming look came over him.

"What would you do, Charles?"

Charles's first thought was that of a newsman, run the story. But then he thought again. The city was a powder keg. The unemployed and the forgotten were wandering the streets, people all over seemed aimless, helpless, or lost. One big panic like this could open up the flood gates. The city could fall into such a state of confusion and terror that the National Guard would be unable to put it back together. Millions of citizens on the rampage. They didn't need much to ignite the sparks. It could be a horrible bloodbath. He thought again, but he found himself without an answer.

Charles was without words. Suddenly, he realized what Rogers had been trying to tell him all along. He put his head down and slowly left the office, leaving the door open. Mr. Rogers faintly regretted the whole incident, as he watched Charles, shaken, walk slowly down the hall, and back to the newsroom.

When Charles got back to the newsroom, Kurt, who had been waiting by the window, signaled Charles over to him.

Charles looked shaken and a bit dazed. His senses had been much too overloaded for one day. So much had transpired. He stared out of the window at the protestors who, screaming and scuffling, were being loaded into tan-like paddy wagons.

"What happened, Charles?" Kurt enquired. "What did he say?"

Charles looked at Kurt. "I don't know, Kurt. Things are so far out of whack. So much has happened to me today. I'm gonna need a little time to sort everything out."

He started back for his desk. Kurt watched Charles for a moment, looked at his watch, and then turned to the window to watch the protestors once more.

Chapter 5
Nineveh's Lot

Despite Kurt's complacency, he was, in fact, a very gifted reporter. He had covered some of the major stories in the city and had done a most professional job. He had a tenacious, inquiring mind.

Kurt looked up into the sky at the cloud formation of the crucifix. He too had noticed it and had wondered what it meant. He'd heard wild rumors concerning its origin and had wanted to track down the reasons for it being there. The cloud pattern was so peculiar as it moved across the sky in an arch, fading into the distance only to be seen again, like a natural could, but then not. But what Kurt could not know was that the mysterious formation held greater meaning than he could fathom, even as he watched in wonder.

The ire of the sign of the cross spanned beyond the borders of Southern California. Even as Kurt watched; its shadow was seen in all parts of the world. The spectator of this mysterious sign cast in the view along the Rockies down through Mexico. Throughout the Midwest, the Eastern Seaboard, and the whole northernmost parts of North America, the misty form of the cross spanned the horizons. Its presence stretched across the Caribbean and the Middle American countries down through South America to the furthest tip of Chile. No one in Northern Europe or in the countries of the Near East knew the sign's origin or meaning, yet its eerie presence was felt. As it arched above Africa and spread an ascending path over Australia, those who noticed pondered for a meaning. The peculiar, almost ominous occurrence, had not escaped the great Russian bear nor the populous dragon of Central Asia, and no one knew the signs that would follow in its wake.

Kurt knew, through small news blurbs on the teletype, that this sign had appeared all over the world. But within the world, in the state that it was, a mere cloud formation took a backseat to the wars, pollution, corruption, and vice plaguing the populations.

He watched the cross arching its path in the sky, slowly, almost imperatively, like the hour hand of a clock. The message obscured, a warning unknown, an ominous sign, a foreboding prediction; the crucifix shadowed a hex on the young and the old, the good and the bad, the just and the unjust alike.

In the streets of Los Angeles below, papers and other litter blew in the warm winds. Urban tumbleweeds in a morally deserted environment. The streets were dirty because many of the garbage men and city sanitary workers were on strike. Various workers were represented by different unions even in the same department, and while one group could be working, another could very well be on strike at any given time.

Abandoned stores, which were looted, attacked by arsonists, or torched for the insurance money, were boarded up or torn down. Vacant lots, strewn with glass, broken bricks and plasterboard, were frequent sites next to functioning businesses. Merchants either hired guards or paid protection to extortionists in order to stay in business. They had bars on their windows in their establishments.

The quest for material goods had everyone on edge, and few citizens felt totally safe. Although many homes looked fortresses, most people were fearful of living alone. There were steel and bard wire fences, iron gates on the doors, bars on every window, and several vicious guard dogs and cats in the yards of some residence.

A siren went off up the block as two stocking-capped bandits ran down the street, stuffing money and jewelry into their opened shirts. The owner of the pawnshop, the victim, stood out in front, shaking up and down in confusion and fear, not knowing whether to chase the two with the gun he'd pulled out; or if he should stay back and further protect the store. He shot the pistol in the air, screaming. The bandits ran down the block, stumbling and knocking people over, as they got away.

Brightly painted ladies in flashy tight-fitting outfits laughed at the scene. These prostitutes crowded the corners and staked out spots from which they would solicit customers. Often, well to do men and women would cruise the neighborhood, seeking offers from these women. Male prostitutes were sparsely mingled among them, but they could be found in mass uptown which was their established territory.

Children, some the unwanted, unloved offspring of the prostitutes, wandered half-naked in the streets, begging passers-by for money. A group of kids ran up an alley with sticks and empty wine bottles, chasing a rat which was furiously scurrying for an abandoned garage. In the alleys alongside the ill-kept tenements and flats, wines and drunks sat on crates. With their bottles rolled up in paper bags; they drank and talked about drinking. Junkies, too far strung out on heroin and a synthetic mix called DS3 lip speed or animal tranquilizers, stood in hallways skin popping or nodding slowly as the sting of their lives floated down the tunnel of their constant escape.

"Hey, baby. Why don't you shake those things over here where I can get a little?" a rather ragged elderly man with a bristly appearance and a filthy scum resembling grease mixed with dirt in his face commented lewdly. He stood hobbling on one leg on a street corner, directing his comments to a very neatly dressed young woman. She tried to ignore him, but when she passed, he reached out and tried to grab her skirt.

"No, you don't, you filthy piece of trash!" the woman shouted in fierce anger and maneuvered out of his reach.

"I'll show you trash," the old man sneered as he pinched his fingers in and out, kissing at the air in her direction.

As she got to a bus stop near the corner, two youths knocked an elderly woman down, grabbing her purse and running in the other direction. A passing cop saw the crime and took off after the youths. While the young woman knelt down to help the older lady, her purse was snapped open by a thinly built pickpocket standing next to the two, and her wallet was lifted lightly, swiftly, and expertly from the purse.

The filthy old cripple on the corner called out to the woman this time to warn her of the pickpocket, but she rebuffed him thinking he was only trying to harass her again. The old cripple had been out on that same corner for years. He had become a permanent fixture in the neighborhood. He'd worked at an elevator company as a younger man, and when he grew close to retirement; he had an unfortunate accident. His leg was caught in a pully and crushed, destroying muscles, tendons and nerves. It was saved from amputation, but he lost all feeling and use of the leg. In time, due to lack of use and working of the muscles, it began to draw up. The company fired him only eleven months before he was to retire on pension, leaving him almost totally without income. The social security system was in shambles and public assistance was taxed beyond capacity. He was forced to live in hallways and sell pencils on the street corners.

The woman helped the accosted elderly lady up on the bus when it arrived; she then got on, and the driver closed the bus door abruptly, before swiftly moving on. As the bus pulled off, the scream of a woman shrieked. It was in a different direction. Women were attacked with great regularity, and many only went out of their homes when they had to. Sex crimes, rapes, and murders were growing daily in number and frequency. Many women carried guns in their purses, and numerous arms instructors taught how to use them when they encountered trouble. Even so, the violence hadn't stopped. Cars drove up and tried to lure young girls and boys going to and from school into them. There were not only crossing guards for the little ones at school but walking guards suspiciously eyed city blocks to help protect them from this sort of assault.

On the steps of a large church in the Hollywood area, four youngsters about the age of thirteen were shooting dice, drinking liquor, and loudly talking. The young boys were rolling off slang, shooting phrases, and clicking together the dice, letting them fall against the steps. Coins were dropping and being picked up off the steps by the bettors who were displaying temper at losing points and money.

An elderly man, who was an established member of the church, passed by the gambling scene and was made upset by the blatant lack of any respect displayed by the youths.

"You kids, stop that! Get away from there! Don't you know better than that? This is a church. Get away from there!"

"Kiss this!" a rude member of the group shouted, grabbing the crotch of his pants. The group laughed.

"You old fart! What difference does this make? You play bingo and bet on racetrack horses in there yourself. If you want to play the old man, play with yourself. Or with all the sissy fagots that get sucked into a rip-off joint like this."

Another of the youths swallowed the last drop of the wine in one of the groups' bottles and threw the container at the old man. It landed squarely on the left side of his head as he turned away in defense. It then bounced once and splattered in the street.

The largest of the youths ran up to him, sweeping the elder off his feet. The old man soon felt a thud in his back, combined with another ache, as a foot stroked across his ribcage. A crushing heel smashed down into his jaw as he heard something make a muffled snapping sound. He felt warm liquid ooze out of his nose and mouth. When the elder tried to push up, he felt the weight of what seemed to be a thousand feet push him back to the ground.

The boys took their fill of the beating, and when the old man couldn't move, the group ran down an alley behind the church, laughing and joking about it. The old man lay still for a moment in shock and pain. All he could think of was that he couldn't open his mouth. He finally did open it and heard a louder pop followed by a loss of control of this lower jaw, causing excruciating pain.

Two blocks over at a Savings and Loan, an old beat-up hearse sat parked on the other side of the street. General Tito Sanchoue, Field Marshall of the Strike Force Wing of the Freedom Party, laid the final plans for the assault on the Savings and Loan. The money was to buy arms to strengthen the party. All the necessary plans had been made. Two female members were to walk in; one was to stay at the door with an automatic Thompson under her coat while another pretended to open an account. Then another would walk in and pretend to faint. In the commotion, the door guard would bolt in, announce the hold-up and lock the doors. In four minutes, they planned to hit the drawers, the safe, and the deposit boxes; after which, the hearse, then in the alley, would collect the group and the tale, leaving the front doors locked. The employees were to be forced into a small teller's stall moments before the Strike Force exited.

The plan progressed smoothly until the decoy went in and fainted, as Sanchoue and the others bolted out of the vehicle across the street. Suddenly, people who were seemingly passers-by, tellers and customers, uncovered themselves and hit the floor in military fashion. They were Special Tactics officers from the FBI and the LAPD. Shots were fired and two of Sanchoue's men were quickly hit. It was a setup. Somebody from inside the organization had tipped them off.

Sanchoue knew he was caught and surrendered immediately. In no time, sirens blaring squad cars converged outside of the landing institution. The getaway men and the driver had no time to escape. They were quickly pulled out of the surrounded hearse and made to spread eagle on the ground with Winchester Pump shotguns pressed tightly to the back of their necks. Suited authorities were buzzing all around the front entrance and inside of the building, taking notes. They smiled and talked to reporters who were there almost instantly. As the scene developed, a large crowd began to gather around the incident.

Sanchoue and his compatriots were gathered together in a line, handcuffed and headed toward an armored caged police vehicle. One of the women in the group began to scuffle and shouted out, "Death to fascism!"

Some of the crowd laughed while others cried the same response back to her.

Sanchoue began to wave his manacled fists in the air.

"All power to the people!" he shouted as he got responses back from the gathered crowd.

The mass of people was getting stirred up by the incident. It was becoming obvious to the authorities that they sympathized with the Freedom Party.

"Down with the fascist pigs!" a bystander shouted.

"Death to fascism," another woman shouted again. She began chanting, "Death to fascism. Death to fascism!"

Sanchoue joined in and soon he had the whole mob chanting with him. The police felt the rising tension and hurried the chained group into the vehicle. There was resistance and squirming as the strike force resisted being placed inside. The scuffling became so intense that an officer unstrapped his baton and took a couple of well-chosen swings at the resisting members. A couple of the members of the crowd broke through in fury and attacked the police officers around the paddy wagon, but were beaten back. The crowd continued to scream obscenities at the police. Finally, the last member of the party was forced onto the wagon and it was whisked away.

Out in front of KGBH Television Station, the last of another chanting mob were being forced into reinforced paddy wagons by police and the station security staff. Kurt's mind drifted as he stood by the window only half-watching the event. He was jolted, however when he heard a loud pop and saw an instant flash of light down near one of the vehicles. The group of resisters inside the bus slouched in their seats, and the enforcement detail around the bus hit the ground. The other onlookers randomly sought cover. There was one lone protestor standing in a tented position shouting a yell while holding the just-fired weapon in his hand. As he shouted, three quick cracks-like sounds came from two prone policemen. The armed man's body violently responded to the jerks of the shells. The protestor hit the pavement and was immediately converged upon by the authorities. They grabbed him off the ground as he limped up on one leg, holding his shoulder. The fight was out of him as he was subdued and thrown bleeding onto the backseat of a police vehicle.

Kurt stood there, stunned by the sheer rawness of the event he'd just witnessed. He thought for a moment how quick and terrible violence seemed to be. Somehow, no matter how much he'd seen of it in his days as a reporter; he could never really fathom it, understand it. He couldn't, and it seemed that nowadays; he was seeing more of it than he ever had before.

As the last paddy wagon pulled off, the one with the wounded protestor, Kurt's eyes followed it up the block. His eyes then focused slowly upward on the cloud formation of the cross hovering on the horizon.

Chapter 6
The Sharing

A golden orange sunset had just cast its warm glisten over the Pacific Ocean as the Kellys family moved about their spacious kitchen and dining room in preparation for their dinner guests. Ann set a beautiful centerpiece of yellow carnations in the center of the table. She touched the pedals around the bottom of the plant, and a beautiful green glow came on. It was a cell powered fixture in the lamp base. The hue changed to aqua and then to blue slowly as it transformed the color of the tablecloth beneath it.

Linda ran up to look at the centerpiece, resting her hands under her chin on the edge of the table. Charles turned and smiled as he noticed the bright color.

"That's very pretty, Ann. Where did you get it?"

"An ad in our charge card billing came last month for this centerpiece. It was so pretty that I mailed for it."

"Are those flowers real?" Charles asked, stepping closer to examine the piece.

Ann laughed, "No dear, they're not."

"But they look so real, and smell so fresh," Charles stated, hardly able to believe it.

"That's why I bought it," Ann quipped, "Teresa's got one and I thought hers was so nice, I couldn't resist."

While Charles looked intently at the flowers and the changing colors, the doorbell rang. Linda ran to the front door and opened it. Charles followed close behind.

"Kurt, Jennifer, come on in," he greeted. He looked down at Tommy, who walked in and began sniffing the apple pie still baking in the oven. Charles knuckled playfully at Tommy's chin.

"You little devil. Already hot for that old apple pie, huh?"

Tommy smiled shyly.

"If I ever hear about an apple pie bandit, I'm going to hire out Tommy as the bloodhound." The four of them laughed as Ann came out of the dining room into the foyer.

"Charles, are you razzing the Lindaquists again?" She put her hands on her hips and mockingly shook her head. "Take their coats. Come on in folks, make yourself at home."

Charles took three coats and hung them in the hall closet. Linda ran upstairs and got her game of dominos. She encouragingly pulled Tommy off toward a corner of the living room. Linda liked to play with Tommy. He was very friendly and was constantly laughing at one thing or another. When the two of them got together, there seemed to be a special sort of communication between them. Dominos was one of their favorite games. Mainly because Linda almost won, which constantly seemed to challenge Tommy.

Ann took Jennifer into the kitchen to help put the finishing touches on the evening's meal. Charles and Kurt went into the living room. Charles flipped on the television. The Kellys had an 'L' shaped front room with a big screen hanging flat-wall television set and a green corner-sectional sofa unit positioned across from the big screen. They had a series of lights in the ceiling which set off the paintings adorning the front room walls. A big picture window at the wide end of the room was highlighted by a large caprice hanging lamp and two comfortable matching chairs in each corner.

Charles picked up the space control module selector and switched to the news on a rival network. Kurt looked at Charles and laughed. It somehow seemed sacrilegious to work for one network's news bureau while, when at home, watching the rival station.

"You could sure singe Rogers's hide with that action, Charles," Kurt joked.

"What do you mean?" Charles defended. "I always watch other stations. Let's me keep abreast of the competition." A rather somber anchorman with a backdrop of clicking typewriters and busy news workers began to pour out the day's events. There were more muggings, arsons, murders, suicides, and scandals. Kurt listened intently in the beginning, but the news was merely the same warmed-over gloom and doom he'd gotten all day on the job. He turned his head with mild irritation and leaned back on the sofa.

"Charles, I don't know how long things can go on like this."

Charles, feeling no different, leaned forward and clicked off the television set. "Yeah. I know what you mean."

He rubbed his hand through his hair and let out a sigh. Kurt could detect an especially weary tone.

"I don't think I can listen to much more today, Kurt. So much has happened to me."

"You mean the Rogers thing?" Kurt added. "I don't think you should worry about that. Rogers likes to blow off a lot of hot air. It'll be forgotten in a few days."

"I don't only mean Rogers's incident. I'm talking about the whole day. I had to cut through town today. I was running late. And Kurt..." Charles paused to collect his thoughts. "You can't believe the state those people were in as we passed through."

"Yes, I hear some of those inner-city people got it pretty tough," Kurt noted mildly.

"Not just tough, Kurt. I've never seen people in such a confused state all my life, even with the news that comes through the station, even though we get to see some gruesome stories. Somehow, when you're not involved, it seems so different. But what I saw today wasn't news flashes, or isolated events, what I saw was mass despair."

Kurt picked up the control and turned on the set again. He began to flick through the numerous stations, looking generally for something interesting.

"I don't know, Kurt," Charles said again. "I can't seem to find the words to put across what I'm trying to say."

Kurt left the set on a natural wildlife feature. He turned and looked at Charles, not really grasping the seriousness Charles was trying to attach to the subject.

"I've seen poverty, Charles. Throughout the country. I don't see what the big deal is. People have always had it bad in the inner city. And while I'd have to admit, it is far worse than I've ever seen it; there's absolutely nothing we can do about it."

"I know, buddy." Charles patted Kurt on the knee. "I'm sorry for getting so serious; it's just that so much has happened to me today."

In an effort to bring on a lighter mood, Charles changed the subject.

"Hey, there's a special on Public Television after dinner at seven-thirty tonight. The World Council of Churches is having a big meeting in Rome. It will be on video delay. Why don't we tune the show in? I hear they are going to be discussing some of the strange things that have been going on these days."

"Is that today?" Kurt asked, half surprised. "I wanted to catch that myself, but I thought it was for next Monday night."

"Nope," Charles answered. "Got it right here in the TV Forum, Seven-thirty tonight."

"Sure, why not?" came Kurt's less than an enthusiastic answer.

The two of them sat there in silence for a moment, only half looking at the wildlife feature. It was kind of awkward. They seemed to be on totally different wavelengths tonight. Kurt perceived Charles to be withdrawn, almost distant, and patronizing in the mood. Charles felt a bit uneasy about Kurt's casual, insensitive attitude. Their whole conversation had a kind of disjointed feeling to it, rather forced. Kurt picked up the TV Forum which Charles had set back down on the cocktail table near the sectional unit. He flipped through a few pages and set it down again. Sliding it over, he noticed what looked like a mechanical metal part mounted on a wooden base. "What's that?" he asked.

Charles looked over at the metal part and smiled as he was reminded of his days in Viet Nam. "That's apart from a replaced carburetor on my old Phantom. I kept it for a moment from my old flying days in Nam."

"Oh, yes." Kurt returned as he toyed with the part. "There are probably a lot of memories in this old part."

"Yes, there are," Charles said. He joined his hands around the nape of his neck and leaned all the way back on the sofa, stretching out his legs. "Viet Nam. I wouldn't have gotten mixed up in that crazy war if it were not for my old man."

"Your old man?" Kurt whimsically remarked. "Didn't you tell me your whole family was military stock?"

"All the way back to my great grandfather. I graduated from Annapolis. Rear Admiral George Taylor Kelly. My father's father was a Colonel in the first world war, and then there's General Kellys himself."

"Your old man?" Kurt interjected.

"My old man. He was General Kellys to everybody. Even our family. Nobody ever called him dad. It was either sir or General Kelly. Yes sir, General Kelly. He had my life mapped out for me before I even learned to walk. I was military material, from a long line of high-ranking officers and officials. I'd go into military school, graduate with honors, become some flunky for some Pentagon hot-shot, personally assigned by General Kellys, of course. And then move up the military ladder.

"He was heartbroken when I refused to go to the Academy after high school. People were rebelling and picketing, talking about a new era. I got caught right up in all of it. Hippies, yippies, revolutionaries, everything seemed to be changing.

"It didn't work out for me though. I jumped out there on my own. Lived in a few dumps. Followed a few hippie type gurus. But I didn't fit. My old man was shocked as I was to see me standing at his front door, crying. I told him I'd changed, that I'd seen the light. We sat up that whole night talking and going over the past.

"I was a changed man after that. My father still wanted me to enroll in the Academy, but I wanted to be where the action was. In less than a year, I'd gone from a pot-smoking beatnik to a gung-ho recruit for the armed forces.

"It was so funny. I went down, signed up. I got my physical. When the results came back, my spirits sank. I was classified 4-F. Flat feet."

Kurt chuckled, genuinely amused by the disappointment.

"Well, how did you get in?"

"Oh, a few people owed my father a favor or two. A couple of strokes of the pen. A minor change in the records and…voilà! Instant soldier. But wouldn't you know that General Kelly's kid couldn't be any ordinary foot soldier? I wound up with the Fifth Fighter Squadron, U.S.A.C., and get this…in reconnaissance."

"You just have to know the right people," Kurt joked.

"Yeah. My father was the right person all right. I remember when I was a kid. I would see him at night coming in from making his rounds. By the time I was 15, I'd lived on U.S. bases all around the world. Japan, the Philippines, West Germany, Taiwan, Korea, the Panama Canal Zone, everywhere. He used to come in, unstrap his gun belt and throw it over the bedpost in his bedroom. Dad looked so big, so massive. And that big gun was the most real thing I'd ever seen. I used to be afraid of him. I don't think I ever really lost that fear. When I was eleven years old, we were stationed in South Korea right after the war. I would wander around the base for hours on end with nothing to do. I saw all the lonely soldiers, stockpiles of military hardware, the screaming and shouting of drill sergeants, and other authorities. It was like being cursed to a ship that would never reach the shore. People getting frustrated, drinking, taking drugs, doing mindless things. And then, on Sunday, we'd all get dressed in our best spiffy shiny outfits and step over to the chapel for the church. Imagine that, here we are in the middle of the overwhelming death, destruction, and misery that the Korean War had caused. All the military police, drugs, hatred, and guns. And on Sunday, everyone paused for one hour to worship a God who stood for peace, goodness, and love. It was a tremendous contradiction."

Kurt sat there, strangely transfixed by Charles's story. It was a side of Charles that he'd never known. And for some reason, right now, Charles was at respite to reveal this dimension of his personality.

"Oddly enough, though, I think it was that every element of my early life that finally allowed me to psychologically break with my father," Charles said, continuing his recollection.

"How so?" Kurt asked quickly, eager for Charles to continue.

"It was at that very base in that very chapel that I met somebody; I have never forgotten. An old cleaning woman. A Korean…Mira. She was educated in missionary schools and spoke excellent English. It was she who gave me my first real taste of what Christianity was really about.

"I wasn't very sports-minded, so when most of the other kids of the enlisted men and officers were playing some game or other; sometimes I'd wander over to the chapel where Mira would be working during the day. She would sit me down and read me stories from the scriptures. She'd tell me about Sampson, Daniel in Lion's den, and the travels of St. Paul, the apostle. Somehow, when she'd tell me these things, it didn't seem like they were coming out of some stuffy old book. She made them come alive for me. I began to see how God loved me and what Jesus had done for me. Those were lovely, lovely times.

"She often lit candles and knelt me down, and we would pray together. She taught me the ten commandments and what being obedient to God's laws meant. But most of all, she ignited a spark in me that had been too long repressed by fear. As I came to sort out the confusion of constantly being on the move and the contradiction of being the general's son, I grasped the first rudiments of my understanding. And suddenly, I had an outlet for all my fear and frustrations. I'd cry on Jesus's shoulder, and I always felt better. Things started working out. Somehow, my life started gaining some sort of order.

"Mira would sit down in the back of the chapel after she was done and tell me about the prophecies of the Bible. About the end time and the second coming of Christ. She told me time was coming when things would seem to happen much faster than they normally might. She said there would be many big and little wars, earthquakes, pestilences, and famine. That these would be the signs of the approaching of the end of time. Mira also spoke of family disunity, suicide attempts, much mental instability, and heart failure. Men's hearts would fail them for the fear of what was about to come on the, she'd say. My open mind drank in every word of her small lessons to me. They were more valuable than going through a thousand Sundays of those formal routines. Even when I got older and moved away from those teachings, they stayed deep inside me. My respect for the power of God never dwindled. Through the rebellion days, the hippie period, my years in Vietnam, down to the day when I broke it to my father that I would not pursue a military career; God was right with me. He ultimately became my courage. That extra push I needed to keep me going when times got rough."

"Dinner is served!" Ann called out from the dining room and broke into the narration of Charles's remembrances.

"He must have taken that pretty hard," Kurt said, rising up to head into the dining room. "Took him a long time to get over it."

"Get over what?" Ann interjected jokingly. "Get over what a great cook you're married to?"

Charles patted his stomach as the two families came to the table. "Almost too good."

"No, I'm serious," Kurt persisted, as he slid out a chair to sit down. "After those uninterrupted years of tradition, it seems like he'd have an awful time adjusting with that kind of break."

"He did, Kurt. He did. But my father was a strong man. Things got him down but he had remarkable resilience. Once he realized that I was serious about it whether he liked it or not; he finally came around. He was one of the people that helped me land my position with the station."

"Can I have some pie?" Tommy, hungry and growing impatient, asked.

"Hold your horses, hungry jack. First things first," his mother responded.

Charles slipped a Bible off the hutch and opened it to a random verse in the scripture, as was his custom to offer this form of grace before eating. The two families bowed their heads. Kurt's more out of respect for Charles than for any feeling of offering a blessing. His family never normally bothered with such things. Charles looked upon the open pages and began reading. "Behold, he is coming with the clouds, and every eye will see him, even those who pierced him, and all the tribe of the earth will mourn over him. Even so Amen."

There were silent moments after the reading. The reading had an odd ring to it. Something about it sounded strange, almost familiar.

"Can I have a piece of pie now?" came Tommy's impatient cry again.

Linda put her hand over her mouth and smiled.

"Mind your manners, young man," Jennifer snapped. "You'll get a piece of pie after dinner! Not before!"

The families then began to pass around the various dishes that had been prepared for the evening's meal. There were corn and potatoes, fresh greens, tossed salad, and smoked ham. The food was delicious and the conversation on the lighter side. The Lindaquists talked about Tommy's musical abilities, and the great progress he was making in school. Charles proudly countered with Linda's budding artistic talent. Jennifer and Ann swapped recipes on Spanish style corn casserole while Kurt helped himself to a second portion of ham. When the dinner was done, the table was cleared, and warm deep dishes of apple pie and vanilla ice cream were served up much to Tommy's delight. He ate hardy and was the only one who asked for a second helping. His mother declined the request once more, scolding him to mind his manners.

When the dessert was over, Linda wanted to help with the dishes, but Ann told her to entertain her company. She and Tommy went back to their dominos after a very satisfying meal.

Kurt and Charles sat at the dining room table, Kurt using a toothpick and Charles flipping pates through his Bible.

With arched eyebrows, Kurt leaned forward in his chair, "Charles," he motioned. "What did Rogers tell you in his office today that made you so upset?"

Charles continued turning the pages of the Bible, not responding for a moment. He then rose up slowly, looking into Kurt's eyes. He was going to tell Kurt about the board meetings. About the decisions to cover-up important news stories. About the wire service confidential. Then he remembered Rogers's words. That he'd already told him more than he was supposed to. He had Rogers's confidence. He couldn't tell Kurt.

Charles then lowered his eyes and covered up. "Just more of the same old thing, Kurt. You know. The same old story. I want to run more hard news while Rogers thought the soft stuff is better for the ratings."

Kurt's reporter instincts took over. He felt somehow that Charles was not being totally straight with him. Rogers and Charles had had that discussion before. No, whatever Charles had been upset about, it had to be more than the hard-soft news issue.

"Come on, Charles," Kurt intoned. "You can tell me. I want to know. Really, what happened in there?"

Charles fell back in his chair. It was useless to try to deceive Kurt. "I can't tell you. I really can't. All I can say is that everywhere, even at the station, things have gotten far out of hand."

Kurt still wanted to know but perceived he was not going to get an answer.

"Hey, it's going on seven-thirty." Charles chimed through the long pause. "Almost time for the special."

Chares got up and walked over to the TV set. The kids had the radio monitor on while they played dominos in the corner. When Charles turned on the set, cutting out the music, they both rose up.

"Daddy's got a special show coming on. You two can play without the radio for a while," Charles explained.

Charles turned on the public television channel and relaxed on the couch. The end of one feature followed by the commercials of the up and coming program was aired. Then a blurb for the disclaimer flashed on the screen for the expected broadcast.

PORTIONS OF THIS PROGRAM WERE FILMED IN LASER MICRO DISC AND EDITED FOR BROADCAST AT THIS TIME.

"Hello. I'm Aaron Forsyth," a British accented commentator began as the broadcast started in.

"This is it, turn it up a little," Kurt stated. Charles adjusted himself on the sofa and pressed the volume button on the space control module.

"In Rome, Italy, the third week of a five-week conference by the World Council of Churches on the special problems of our day began. The meeting was presided over by Monsignor Yosef Antonio St. Martin. Members of the body included high ranking bishops and officials from throughout the world. The role of the Church today is in a state of transition. All over the world, people are experiencing problems never before faced by a society so modern as ours."

"As in the past, the Church concerns itself mainly with moral and social issues. The plight of the poor, giving council to the wayward and providing missionaries to the more remote areas the planet. But now, we see a whole new social crisis of the caliber never faced by any society before us. The Church is interested in identifying specific social ills, their symptoms, and causes. The conference representatives then plan to make an attempt to address these concerns."

The commentator then went into an interview with a local church authority on the subject at the studio. They talked about the widening gap between rich and poor, and about the strange physical signs that kept cropping up everywhere. They disagreed on the causes of such events and discussed the overall impact it was having on Church bodies and organizations. When the short interview had ended, the meeting in Rome was switched into the monitors.

There were the hushed muffled voices of the large mass of people assembled for the conference. The attire of the different members ranged from the black outfits with white collars worn by some of the more conservative denominations to the bright colored embroidered outfits worn by the more traditional clergy.

The conference chambers were a highly official-looking multi-seated room with dark wooden trim and deep red carpeting. In the center was an elevated podium with a large eight-seat chamber placement and a speaker's box in the very middle of that. The perimeter was lined with glass booths filled with interpreters wearing headsets, tuned into the various delegates for language translations.

A gavel was sounded, and the random voices and paper shuffling noises faded out at the sound of the monsignor's voice.

"May the Lord shed his blessings on this third week of our conference addressing the problems and the needs of the people of the world. May we open with a prayer from the chancellor seated to my right."

The chancellor got up and offered up a broad prayer, seeking blessing for the members of the council and to all the people of the world. This was followed by the saluting recognition of the World Council of Churches elected officials' announcements and preliminary discussions. The itinerary and minutes were handed out to every committee and caucus from the preceding weeks. Then an order was given to open the floor for the meeting's discussion.

A clerical diplomat rose. A bishop from the Anglican Church in Central Africa. Interpreters for the other members tuned in and began to translate the message of Africa who spoke in his native tongue.

"Good people at this conference. I represent the congregation of the states of West and West-Central Africa. We are a small body compared to some, but our work is singularly important. Many of my constituents occupy lands where industrialization has not made a significant impact. These people are very close to the earth. Many still live in straw huts, and hunting is their source of support. These villagers watch the habits of the animals very closely.

"Reports have come to my attention over the past few months of very unusual behavior by most of the animals. Normally, in times of excessive dryness, many animals migrate close to water holes opposite the direction of the impending drought. The hunters are observing such strange preparatory behavior when no drought seems to be influencing it. There are also accounts of animals storing food and not wandering, as was their nature and habit for thousands of years. This is in conjunction with the decrease in fertility rates and an increase in mental disorders among the villagers. I have come to the feeling that these events are related."

The monsignor thanked the diplomat for his observations. He then opened the floor for discussion or additions to the African diplomat's viewpoints. A red light flashed on the podium as a cardinal from France signaled his desire to speak. When they indicated that the French cardinal had the floor, some delegates put on their earphones to be assisted by interpreters in the outer chambers.

"I give honor to you, Monsignor, and to this great assembly of clergy. This is momentous and at the same time, a sad occasion. France, as you know, is one of the leading industrial powers in the world. We are a nation rich in cultural heritage. We are the nation of Napoleon, Pasteur, Charles De Gaulle, and yet our homicide rate is up, our suicide rate is up, our citizens pay hundreds of millions out in fees to psychiatrists and psychologists. Strangeness is in the air over our lands as well. People report seeing strange sights in the skies. Plants and animals are displaying unusual behavior. Our people cry out for moral decency. For a return to a time when man cared for his fellow man."

"If we, as a human race, could become more sensitive to each other. If we would show compassion and have the force of God in our lives. We could begin to make the journey back. I think we, in reference to the whole human body, have gone too far searching for the answers to questions that should never have been asked in the first place. That incapacity to know. We have documented biblical prophetic scripture that one day a man would reach this point. I am personally awed by the bizarre events that have taken place worldwide as of late. My only question as I look around me is. Has time run out?"

There was a stirring from the delegation as the various members were ruffled by the raw question from the French cardinal. The monsignor pounded his gavel to restore order to the muffled voices in the assembly.

"We must be reminded…" he stated over the last few voices setting down, "we must be reminded that these views are the expression of the individual members only and not the official opinion of this council."

There were a few more hushed voices while Monsignor leaned over and took a message in his ear from the page. He then raised the gavel once more, silencing the group. After a few seconds pause, he signaled for the Argentinean Bishop of a Synod of the Lutheran faith to have the floor.

The bishop was a small man in his seventies. He moved very slowly and talked with great concentration. The non-Spanish speaking delegates switched over to the special interpreters when the bishop began to speak.

"Monsignor St. Martin, Bishop Spielman, Cardinal Andolini and the members of the Anglican delegation, you all know me, we have worked together closely for many years. That is why I must say what I must say. In our large Latin American nation, more has happened in the last two years to drive an evil wedge into the people than has happened in all the years the country has existed. My people, bonded together by strong family ties and traditions, are growing weak. Children, little ones, five years, even three, are becoming addicted to drugs. Those once strong family ties are breaking down. The daughter turns her hand to her mother, son to the father. I would be the last to say this were it not true. But this body, the Church, seems powerless to stem the tide which is coming upon us."

There was another roar of disapproval as some of the members of the council were becoming outraged by the statements being made.

A vice-chancellor of an important district of the West Germany Methodists signaled and rose, demanding to have the floor. He was immediately given permission to speak by the presiding officer.

"Monsignor, with all due respect to the great assembly of clergymen from the four corners of the earth, I implore you, these ramblings by my very well-respected colleagues are rather nothing but confused utterances. I hardly consider a group of underdeveloped villagers to be experienced zoologists or botanists, and in reference to the reason for the increase in social disturbance; I think it is a matter of conjecture to blame it on some impending doom. The religious bodies represented here who would bring into question the very notion of a quote end of time unquote. I think some of the problems brought under consideration at this conference demand further study. I think it would be highly irresponsible to simply access these complex events to some sort of spiritual mumbo jumbo."

There was some laughter from some in the group at the final comment from the vice-chancellor, followed by the loud chatter of the disagreeing factions of the delegations over the controversy. The monsignor called out for members of the Eastern European, European, and North American delegations to meet with him in a special chamber set up for such mini-conferences. He then pounded the gavel and called for a fifteen-minute recess while the delegations conferred. Back at the studio, Mr. Forsyth, the commentator, and the guest minister, made comments on the portion of the meeting that had transpired.

Charles had wanted to view the entire program, but he felt himself getting drowsy throughout the broadcast. Kurt, seeing nothing that he felt of particular interest in this meeting which had already taken place, used the recess as an opportunity to slip into the kitchen for a cold drink.

He came out moments later arm in arm with Jennifer. Ann followed them and sat next to Charles on the sofa. She noticed his tired expression and clicked off the television.

"Don't turn that off," Charles tried to demand, not really putting up much of a fuss, "I was watching that."

"You're nearly dead to the world," Ann said. "You've had a rough day. We all have."

"Ain't that the truth," Kurt added.

"Have you been able to track down any information on Linda's problem?" Jennifer asked, almost in passing.

Ann shrugged her shoulders, "Information I have, tons of opinions and ideas. What I need are facts. So far, nobody's seen their way clear to slow down long enough to give me any. You know, doctors are so into themselves these days that sometimes I think we ought to junk the AMA and go back to fold medicine."

"Ah, but it's too late, Ann," Jennifer interjected. "It costs so much to provide a medical education now that only the elite can afford one. It was sheer destiny that doctors would wind up in the area where everything else seems to be going these days. Into the hands of the rich."

"Well, they better look over their shoulders or pretty soon they're going to price themselves clean out of sight," Kurt added. "I heard about an accident this morning where the victim didn't have any insurance or any means to pay for medical help. When the ambulance got there and the paramedics found out, they just propped him up on the curb and left him there.”

“How awful?” Ann turned her head away in genuine disgust. “What happened to the poor man?”

“I don’t know.” Kurt shrugged his shoulders. “But at that rate, the rich are going to end up only treating themselves.”

“It would serve them right,” Jennifer interjected.

Ann turned to Charles, who was dozing off on the couch even in the midst of the conversation. Ann stroked his cheek and looked lovingly on him. “Poor dear, he’s really had a rough day today.”

“Linda,” Ann called out. The slight rise in her voice snapped Charles out of the doze. “Put up the game and let’s get Tommy ready to go.”

“Was I asleep?” Charles added groggily. “I’m sorry. I was trying to watch that program.”

“Ease on back buddy, we’re about ready to pull out,” Kurt said.

Charles stood up, stretched, and yawned, rubbing his eyes as the two families walked toward the hall closet.

“Sorry, I lost you for a minute there, Kurt. I didn’t realize I was that tired.”

The Lindaquists put on their coats. Linda kissed Tommy on the cheek. A surprised Tommy blushed at the show of affection.

“Don’t worry about it, Charles. You catch a full eight hours, and you’ll be as good as new in the morning.”

Jennifer hugged Ann as Kurt opened the front door. the Kellys stood in the doorway and waved to the Lindaquists as they climbed into their luxury sedan and pulled out of the driveway. They then returned to the living room and picked up a few scattered things, put them into their places, and turned in for the night.

Chapter 7
Eve of the Messenger

The Kellys family slowly descended the short stairway to their dining room in pajamas and robes this early morning hour. The sun had been up for only a short time, and the family had come down for a morning devotional. Charles had been conducting a morning devotional for more than a year now after he'd read a tract from the Moody Bible Society which had suggested the idea. The tract stated that families throughout the country who had engaged in such activities of faith had grown closer. Husband and wife once reconciled to God each morning to develop a direct line to working out daily problems. Children to each family, by the example of their parents, also seemed to gain better adjustment from the experience.

This habit the family routinely went through almost every morning. But when conditions around the world grew increasingly less stable and times got harder, there seemed to be a greater intensity of self-application during the little service.

Charles led his family in prayer as the three of them bowed in worship. He then reached for his Bible to select a scripture for the morning's service. He set the Bible on the table, and it flipped upon to a chapter he had not intended to read. Charles started to turn the page, but the words at a glance caught his eye and he was drawn to them. He read a little more and could not turn away. He then began reading aloud from Matthew chapter twenty-four and verse three.

"As He sat upon the Mount of Olives, the disciples came unto him privately, saying tell us, when shall these things be? And what shall be the sign of thy coming and of the end of the world? And Jesus answered and said unto them, take heed that no man deceive you for many shall come in my name saying I am Christ; and shall deceive many. And ye shall hear of wars and rumors of wars. See that ye not be troubled: for all these things shall come to pass but the end is not yet.

"For nation shall rise against nation and kingdom against kingdom: And there shall be famines, and pestilences, and earthquakes in diverse places. All these are the beginning of sorrows then shall they deliver you up to be afflicted, and shall kill you: and you shall be hated of all nations for my names sake. And then shall many be offended and shall betray one and other and shall hate one another. And many false prophets shall rise, and shall deceive many and because iniquity shall abound. The love of many shall wax cold. But he that endure unto the end, the same shall be saved."

After Charles read the scripture, there was a long moment of silence. The scripture had a strange ring to it, much like the reading at last night's dinner. Linda pressed her hands hard together, tightened her closed eyes and a tear ran down her face as she prayed even harder after the scripture. Ann looked at Linda, taken by her apparent intensity. She looked at Charles, who was equally surprised by their daughter's behavior.

Charles then offered up a closing prayer of thanksgiving and ended the devotional, but he almost had to pull Linda from her chair, reminding her that she had school to attend today. Linda heard and slowly got up from the table.

Charles patted Linda on the bottom, "Go up and get ready for school."

Linda ran upstairs and went into her room, getting out the gold and blue jumper to her school uniform.

Ann went into the kitchen, pulling out three prepared trays of waffles and Canadian bacon from the refrigerator. She placed them in the radar range, set the timer, and glanced at Charles, who was standing with his arms folded leaning in the doorway. Ann noticed his preoccupation in thought, but she was not alarmed by it.

She then returned to the refrigerator and took out a gallon bottle of mineral water, pouring three glasses around the small breakfast table in the kitchen.

"Did you notice Linda?" Charles asked in a disturbed voice.

"Yes, I did," Ann answered. "She seemed so intense. So completely immersed in this morning's prayer."

"But you know, honey? I felt somehow moved by that reading too. What made you pick that scripture?"

"I don't know," came Charles's somewhat confused reply. "I hadn't intended to read that, but when I saw it in passing, I couldn't turn away."

Ann pulled back the kitchen curtains and tried to peek at the sky. Barely over the roof of the house at the very tip of her vision, she caught a glimpse of the crucifix arching slowly across the sky.

"Is it still there?" Charles enquired, knowing exactly what Ann was looking for.

"Uh-huh. Like the moon itself. There it is, plain as the sun, in broad daylight."

Charles put the back of his thumb over his mouth in thought and then began to shake the hand downward in a pattern. The shaking predicted his coming to some overall conclusion. He then walked over to the sink.

"That cross," he began, this time pointing his finger, "that cross is definitely a part of the peculiar things going on. I'm sure of it. Out of all the inconsistencies that have going on, the fact of the cross has been the most consistent."

"I don't know. I got the feeling this morning during our devotional that something very unusual is about to happen. Something that somehow will make a profound difference in things."

Ann nervously trembled at the thought. "Charles," she said, her eyes beginning to well up; these were not tears but the emotion of fear. "I'm frightened. I got the same feeling too. It's like a cold dart gripped my heart when you read that passage. I'm afraid, Charles."

"Then we both felt the same thing," Charles said. He turned; Ann followed, to see Linda silently, intently, watching them. Her smile was a faint but confident one. They had not known how long she'd been there. Looking upon her, she looked very far away. Almost like a total stranger.

Beeeeeeeeep! The low humming noise of the radar range sounded a lending warning that the waffles were done. The noise broke the momentary silence, snapping Ann to attention. She quickly went over to the range and with a couple of mitts, pulled the hot waffles out and set them on the kitchen table.

"Come on in Linda. Sit down and eat some nice hot waffles and Canadian bacon. Charles? Do you want any butter?"

Ann started to act busy, playing the housewife role in an effort to dissuade her fears. She went to a strange cabinet and frantically got down a small jar of maple syrup. She then titled the skillet containing the bacon over in her rush to fix the plates. Nervously, she reached over the sink for paper towels. While she looked around during the cleanup, Charles grabbed her hand and held it firm.

"Ann," he said, looking earnestly into her eyes. "Slow down. You've got everything."

Ann paused suddenly, realizing her unusually rapid movements. She then sat, took a sip of water, and tried to compose herself.

When the family had finished eating breakfast, the three of them harmoniously washed the used utensils. Linda was then left to go over her school lessons while Charles and Ann went upstairs to get dressed for work.

Ann fumbled through the closet to pick out the day's uniform. Charles, who was already wearing his suit pants, picked up buff to shine his black shoes.

"Ann, why does the idea of change frighten you?" Charles casually looked up and asked from his brushing.

"It's not that," Ann answered, combing her hair. "I don't simply fear change. I know things can't go on the way they have been. It's the unknown element that upsets me. How can we be sure a situation worse than the one we are in is not in the offing? How can we be sure that the pent up force of those people in the inner city might not one day become unhinged? You saw their hate. Their rage. Granted, we're blessed, Charles. But for every family like us, there are a thousand not so fortunate."

Charles sat on the end of the bed with a disturbed expression on his face. Buttoning a blue shirt he'd put on; he spoke slowly. "Why fear, Ann? We have done nothing wrong. We both work hard and try to take advantage of opportunities. We take from no one. Our life is not complicated. We give to charities, help out when we can. Ours is not to question the blessings we have been given. Only to take care of and do the right things. And no matter how bad things get, we can feel secure in the knowledge that we did our part. That being done, we can prepare for our portion of our inheritance that God's new kingdom promised. No more can be expected."

Ann put her head down, adjusting her white belt at the waist. "I know, Charles. I feel a little better now." A smile began to show on her face. "After all, it was merely a feeling. I get feelings all the time."

"Don't give it another thought," Charles reassured. "Remember, Christ said how many of us through worry can add even one cubit of our stature."

Ann nodded and smiled in agreement.

The Kellys family came out of the front door. Charles turned to lock it while Ann and Linda went over and got into the Chevy Spyder parked in the drive. Charles walked over and kissed Ann.

"I'll call you at lunch," he said.

Ann tapped the horn as she pulled out of the driveway, turning down the block. Linda waved at her father.

Charles got in his V.W. for the drive to work. En route, he thought about the incidents which had transpired that morning. Could there be a connection between the unusual events of late and the feelings his family was having? Or could the anticipatory atmosphere be a coincidence? There were no authorities. No one he could ask. No one knew any more about it than he did. And yet he could not explain why he felt so anxious. He only knew that he did.

Charles pulled past the large metal plated letters KGBH and up the spacious winding drive to the studio front doors. He got out of his car and was immediately approached by the valet.

"Good morning, Charles."

Charles nodded. "A little more breathing room with the protestors gone."

"Did you have any word on what they did with them?" Charles enquired.

"Booked some, let some go. It's always the same thing. They'll be back in a few weeks. Only next time, it'll be for something else."

Charles shook his head and went up the steps. As he straightened his tie and stepped into the building, he noticed the security guard seemed a lot calmer without the threat of the protesters. He turned and looked at the boarded-up front window where the brick had been thrown the day before.

"Good morning, Mr. Kellys. Sure, it is a fine day," the security guard greeted.

"No protesters," Charles mused.

The security guard smiled and handed Charles the sign-in sheet. "I heard you and Rogers were going at it yesterday. It amazes me how you persist in confronting him. Everybody knows Rogers will never change. When he thinks he's right, boy, forget it."

Charles shrugged his shoulders. "Somebody has got to keep after him."

Taking the elevator, Charles got off on his floor. As he hit the main newsroom, it was in a flow of almost constant motion. Like a little anthill with every individual knowing his part. The world was in a constant state of transformation, and to monitor the world changes, the news bureau at KGBH had its finger on the pulse.

"Charles!" one reporter shouted out from across the room. He wore a shirt and a brown wool vest, his sleeves were rolled up, and he had a pencil and numerous papers in his hand. "I need some help on this White House press secretary story. If you got a minute."

"Let me sit down and get situated," Charles replied. The reporter only wanted to hear a yes, and when Charles didn't respond that way; he waved him off with a snappy hand motion. Putting the pencil in his mouth, the young man looked back on the sheets he was holding.

Charles got to his desk and sat his briefcase on top. He clicked open the lock and opened it in an effort to review some research material before picking up the day's assignments. As he sorted through the papers, he began to run across several popsicle sticks tied together in the shape of crosses.

"How did they get there? What did they mean? Who had placed them there?"

"You're in big trouble now, Charles," whispered a worker passing by, "Here comes Rogers."

Charles shifted his shoulders back and forth, his attention momentarily interrupted between the crosses and the passing worker.

"Charles, good morning," Bernard Rogers said gruffly. Rogers noticed the popsicle sticks in Charles's hands and arched his eyebrows.

Charles smiled shyly. "A joke," he stammered hiding the crosses between folders in the briefcase swiftly closing the top down.

"Of course," Rogers dismissed. "When you get a minute, come down to my office. I've got something going today. A hot one. You'll like this one, Charles."

"I'll be there, Raymond. Right after I get through doing…us…something."

Rogers looked at Charles suspiciously. He then shrugged his shoulders, shaking his head. "Right."

When Rogers turned and headed for Melvin LaClair's office, Charles raised the briefcase again and examined the crosses. He moved his briefcase and laid two of the crosses out on his desk. As he focused on them, he began to get the same feeling he'd gotten earlier, only stronger. While he contemplated the crosses, Kurt walked up.

"Charles, old man. Did you get enough sleep last night?"

Charles did not respond. He continued to stare intently at the crosses. Kurt noticed his intensity and began to look at the crosses himself trying to figure out whatever it was that Charles was focusing on.

"Are you alright?" Kurt asked after being unable to perceive what the importance of the crosses was focusing on.

"Kurt?" Charles asked, holding up one of the crosses. "Does this remind you of anything?"

Kurt looked more at Charles than at the sticks and shook his head. He was almost unnerved by Charles's unusual behavior. Standing up abruptly, Charles walked around several desks and over to the window. He compared the sticks to the image crossing the sky in his eye's view. Kurt walked over to the window, observing Charles's unusual behavior.

"Are you looking at that cloud again, Charles? You're becoming obsessed with this thing." Kurt's words had a scolding twinge to them. "You really haven't been acting yourself lately. I think you've been working too hard. You need a vacation."

Kurt spoke his insecurities of Charles with blind openness. His complacent nature began to show through. He felt secure in Charles remaining the same always. As he had always known him. But Kurt could not accept Charles's changing or any deviation in his character. Charles was reaching out. Acting on perception, he was trying to sort out the puzzles that were confronting himself and his family. But all Kurt could see was Charles's unusual behavior, the behavior he couldn't accept.

"I just came off a vacation," Charles said bluntly, stepping in front of Kurt and walking back to his desk, not waiting for a reply.

Putting the crosses back into the briefcase, Charles sat it under his deck and left the office, striding slowly down the hallway. He knocked twice on Rogers's door and entered. Rogers wasn't there. Charles closed the door behind him and sat down in the chair opposite the desk. He picked up a couple of photographs of Rogers's grandkids, scanning their faces inquisitively. Two smiling girls with wide eyed grins and large braces on their teeth. Charles placed the pictures down in their exact spot; he then began to survey the walls of the cluttered office. There were award plaques from most areas of news coverage. Wire service commendations, magazine foreign bureau chief, broadcast journalism, newspaper reporting, even editorial excellence. Bernard Raymond Rogers was a very distinguished man. A point, Charles lightly thought, he'd like to attain someday. He then got up and edged his way around the side of the desk, sitting down abruptly. Charles was startled and his first reaction was to bolt out of the chair.

"Don't get up," Rogers said. "You stay there while I got out and pick up the story."

Charles said nothing but slowly made his way around the desk, lighting up a cigar. "I put my ideas on the arms race segment to Winston Morganbessor. He's the issues chairman of our commitment, not to mention being a vice president of this end of the company."

"Well," Charles asked, "what did he say?"

"He loved it!" Rogers boomed out. "He thought it was a big idea. He wanted us to start putting the package together right away."

Rogers reached his note holder and pulled off a sheet of paper.

"Out near Barstow at Edwards Air Force Base, we have an inside line on some new equipment being tested this afternoon. We couldn't have timed the whole thing any better. Normally, the press can't get in for the briefings, but your father still has a few old friends. Do you remember Desmond Koening?"

"The name sounds familiar," Charles said.

"Well, Major Koening still remembers you. He said he'd give you a slight tour, but I have to promise not to run the findings before the first of the year."

"Why me, Raymond?" Charles asked.

Rogers smiled warmly. "Because I think you had a little something to do with this. You know your way around the military, and because you are our best reporter."

Charles stood up, feeling a sense of duty, "I'll try to do my best, Raymond."

Rogers scribbled his signature on a yellow slip of paper and handed it to Charles. "You'll need a pass to get over there. Take one of the choppers."

Charles took the pass, smiled at Rogers, turned, and left for his newsroom desk. When he got back to the large busy room, Kurt met him at the door.

"What's happening, Charles?"

"I got an assignment out at Edwards Air Force Base. I'm gonna hit it in the chopper."

"Edwards?" Kurt screamed. "That's supposed to be my beat. I always cover the desert region stories!"

"Sorry, old chum," Charles replied.

He briskly made it to his desk and grabbed his briefcase, tape recorder, and a few other miscellaneous items. In a moment, he passed Kurt, who stood disappointed by the water cooler. After a sharp eye exchange, Charles was on his way to the elevator.

Charles got out of the elevator at the service exit and walked up the remaining flight of stairs to the roof helicopter. When he opened the door, the warm air was calm. The sky showed a bright haze through the pollution filled covering. Charles walked across the landing strip past two choppers and entered a glass-enclosed wait station. He handed his pass to a middle-aged attendant dressed in a white jumpsuit and worker's cap with a microphone extended around his chin.

"They've phoned the clearance up already, Charles," the attendant said. "I've got Harry prepping number six for you."

Charles nodded acknowledgment. He sat down with his briefcase placed on his knees. Opening it, he once again peered at the stick crosses that had worked their way out of his folder. Charles was struck by the same feeling again. He closed his eyes shut and the briefcase.

Soon, he heard the fluttering swishing sound of the helicopter blades settling in over the landing pad.

"This is it," the attendant said energetically.

Charles got up and walked out the glass door into the swirling gusts that the blades were made. Charles held his briefcase right to his chest while he made his way over to the chopper's cockpit.

Harry stuck out his hand in greeting, Charles clasped it firmly.

"Good luck with it, Charles. It's ready to go."

Charles climbed aboard moments after Harry jumped off. Strapping himself in, he began to read the instruments.

"Watch out for this machine," Harry shouted, leaning forward. "If you feel it getting away from you, hold on to it. I gave it a little extra throttle."

"She was kind of sluggish before," Charles shouted in the breezy gusts.

"Don't worry, she's alright now," Harry concluded.

The attendants got each side of the lift circle and chopper to ascend slowly. The forward thrust of the helicopter whisked it into the light swift side motion, and then it steadied effortlessly. Charles hit the switch on his air command, "Number six, okay."

"You're clear, number six. Have a good trip," came the attendant's salutation.

The chopper rose against the day sky. Soon, Charles leveled the craft at a comfortable altitude, moving in a north-easterly direction. He sat back, relaxed for the trip ahead of him.

Chapter 8
The Appearing

The chopper cut effortlessly through the great expanse above the metropolis, pushing toward the mountain ranges. Charles again pressed the throttle inward to gain more altitude, and it responded quickly upward and through the spacious skies.

It was an exhilarating feeling to move so swiftly and effortlessly about with the slightest movement of the hand. Looking around him Charles saw not another craft in the sky. He was the only one. There was something highly stimulating about soaring so high above everything in such a care-free manner. The helicopter was handling with ease just as Harry had said. Charles maneuvered a few sewing patterns for the fun of it; the chopper sailing beyond the city limits.

With more distance between himself and the city, Charles was able to see the Los Angeles areas as more of a basin. The huge grayish clouded landscape was littered with structures and lines of streets there was a depressing haze of mist engulfing the entire area like a bowl filled with smoke. The Los Angeles smog was so thick; it resembled an entirely different atmosphere.

How could people breathe this stuff? Charles thought. It was no wonder the Indians of the region called Los Angeles 'The Big Smokey Valley'.

The density of the smog lessened the further the chopper moved from the valley. The increased visibility was as a curtain unveiling before Charles's eyes. There on the horizon of his eye line, at the outer reaches of his vision, fifteen hundred feet up, and approaching swiftly and as melodically as a soaring condor, Charles took in the panorama of the mountain peaks touching the sky. His eyes lit up and a faint accidental smile concerned his mouth. The overwhelming majesty simply overcame him. The calm air being stirred by the chopper blades, the dispersed wind being pushed by the streamlined chopper, his own sense of freedom, his feeling the power of the rushing engines and the wind glorious view of the largest of all the earth's features brought on more excitement and grandeur than Charles could contain.

What a wonderful maker God must be. What a glorious sight to behold for one so fragile as a man. *The very ability to witness such tremendous landscape was a miracle in itself,* Charles thought. *And yet it was appreciated by a few.*

Charles recalled the gateways he and his family would take into the vast nature of the Western State. From Southern California, they had access to the ocean, deserts, the mountains, and vast valleys. But most of the state's citizens never left the big cities of the San Francisco Bay Area, Los Angeles or San Diego to absorb the varied beauty often only minutes away from them. It was too easy for a person to get caught up in the modern hustle and bustle of those massively populated centers. Everyday survival demanded so much physical or emotional energy that the wonders of nature surely got lost in the shuffle. Many people were simply too frustrated or too busy to venture out.

This seemed to Charles to be a reason why men went astray. How they drifted away from God. Life had become such a painful tedious struggle for so many that they forgot the Creator of all things and concentrated solely on their ills. *This,* he thought, *happened gradually over a period of years, but regardless of the duration of the process, the outcome seemed painfully clear.* The more men concerned themselves with themselves, the less time they had to knowledge the Creator, and all off is natural wonders.

Sailing beyond the mountain ranges, Charles offered a short prayer of thanksgiving to God for his many blessings. He brought the helicopter over the edge of the back slopes and the foothills and could begin to see some of the white sands of the desert off in the distance. He veered a little more toward the north and checked his instruments. He was headed in the direction of Mirage Lake; a prehistoric water site that had long since dried up and became part of the desert. The treetops and sparse foliage at the foot of the desert area looked like broccoli tips from so high up. The air was so still, and everything seemed so motionless and serene that Charles decided to flutter down close enough to send a gentle breeze through the leaves and watch the subtle tree sway from the chopper gusts. The chopper descended to treetop level swiftly, quietly. Charles watched the green foliage under him flutter gently as he looked behind him and smiled. The trees shifted lightly disturbed by the displaced air.

While Charles was moving, he heard a dull thud from above him. It was like a force of air from the ground up, popping as if reaching beyond the narrow end of an invisible funnel. The pop felt like suction and Charles felt the chopper come to a sudden halt. The engines drove harder, but the chopper could move no further. An invisible barrier seemed to be holding it still. The shock of what was happening left Charles's mind reeling. He began to notice the air change beneath him. Looking around, he saw thermos waves that displaced the very air they were cutting through. The thermos waves resembled the wavy streams that emanate from a sun-scorched road on a hot day, only these currents crept toward the chopper from every direction in an instant. When the thermos waves shot under and around the helicopter, Charles heard another muffled thump, like the shutting of some huge padded door. Suddenly, the force from the seismic thump pressed against his entire body. Charles was pipped back in the seat of the chopper. The effect felt as if a thousand pounds had been thrust upon him all at once. He could not breathe under the pressure, but oddly, he felt no oxygen deprivation. The instruments of the helicopter were reading wildly as Charles, under the severe strain, looked up and saw ominous, frightening darkness envelop the skies. It was chilling darkness that he could actually feel.

Charles felt his shirt binding him and he tried to force his pinned hands upward to relieve the biding pressure. Perspiration began to roll down his face, and Charles felt a peculiar burning sensation in his eyes. Squinting to clear his vision, the water welling up in his eyes, he saw a straight line of light like a sharp lightning bolt, only much clearer and a hundred times brighter, force its way through the vacuum created there. The piercing light penetrated through in a continuous charge of illumination and hit the ground in the flashing of an instant, in a clearing just beyond the trees. In the microsecond that the light touched the ground, the thermos condition disappeared. The helicopter burst out of control, spinning round and round above the trees.

Charles grabbed hold of the control and grappled feverishly to bring the chopper under control. It spun wildly for a few seconds but began to level out under Charles's control as the dark sky gradually began to lighten. Charles in pulling the chopper under control looked in the direction where the light has struck and seen a strange image in the clearing. Breathing heavily with frightened eyes and tears streaming down his face Charles fixed on the image in awing disbelief.

With great intent, he aimed the helicopter toward the clearing and tried to force it down on the desert sands. The overcast sky filled with blowing sand made visibility almost impossible. Charles landed a good fifty feet from the figure and staggered out of the helicopter, headed in the strange image's direction.

"Who are you? What has happened? Where did you come from?"

Charles stumbled forward, hollering loudly while waving his arms over his eyes to try to keep the sand from blinding him. The farther he got from the chopper, the better he could see.

"Who are you?" Charles repeated. "Where did you come from?"

He stumbled within ten feet of the figure and could begin to make out some features. They were those of an injured man. The desert was silent to his questions as the man tried to stand but the visibility shook, he fell on his first two attempts. When he stood up on his third attempt, he walked slowly toward Charles. He held out his punctured hands and in a deep steady tone, one that swelled of directness and importance in Charles's ears, the newcomer spoke.

"Fear not me, man. Doubt not what you see. I am a witness and am come to bear a certain passage. Behold a Messenger."

Charles looked at him and slowly put his hands inside the Messenger's. Charles was still trembling in contrast to the composure of his sudden visitor. The Messenger was a young olive complexioned man of very pronounced features. He spoke with an accent that sounded clearer than English. He seemed to be somewhere in his early thirties and his dark clear eyes were vast and knowing. The curly brown head of hair and beard framed a face that aroused contentment in Charles merely by looking upon it.

Charles glanced at the slight trickle of blood in the visitor's hands. He immediately began to fumble in an effort to help the man. He took off his jacket and ripped the blue cotton shirt off his back, tearing it into strips to wrap the Messenger's wounds.

"There is no need," the visitor spoke softly, without emotion.

Charles disregarded the statement and began to wrap the Messenger's wounds, the stranger calmly watching.

"I gotta get you taken care of," Charles nervously chattered. "You need help, and I'm going to make sure you get some."

He tied off the knots in the shredded cloth on both of the Messenger's hands and started to help him over toward the helicopter which whirled noisily in the spot he'd left it. As they made their way toward the chopper, Charles had to lift his arm again to protect his eyes, while the Messenger walked calmly and straight through the swirls of sand without any apparent discomfort. The Messenger, who was dressed in a loose flowing suit of sackcloth that appeared to be one piece with a light rope at the waist and sandless on his feet, climbed up onto the chopper, being helped by Charles, then strapped him into his seat, climbed in on the other side, and lifted the chopper up flying in the direction of the mountains.

Charles was very nervous and excited. He checked several times to see if the Messenger was strapped in tightly. The confusion of the event, plus a thousand questions swirled in Charles's mind. He had to have some answers.

"Who...who are you?" Charles blurted out.

The Messenger remained silent, calmly without motion for a few moments.

They passed over the field of trees where Charles had encountered the mysterious disturbance and headed on toward the mountains.

“As I have said. So am I. I am a Messenger come.”

“Come? Come from where? What message do you bring?” Charles asked in haste between focuses on his instrumental brings.

Chapter 9

A Stranger's Welcome

"KNJR-769 permit KGBH number six requesting clearance for an emergency landing. Over."

Charles signaled on his remote to the ground command of the trauma unit on the landing roof of the Los Angeles Medical Center.

"Stand by," an attendant stated through an intercom as she ran the I.D. through central computer and flashing instantaneously on the screen was the verification. The computer automatically put in a call to KGBH ground control to inform of arrival.

"You have our clearance number six," came back the response from the control booth. "Set down circle three. Circle three," the instructions came firmly.

As the chopper descended, two emergency attendants rushed out into the landing area.

"Hey! Isn't that the KGBH news helicopter?" the taller one said in surprise.

"What in the hell is he doing coming here?" his partner responded in question.

The attendants guided Charles down and centered him on the proper spot. He was excited and winded as he motioned the attendants toward the Messenger who was sitting calmly in the next seat. Leaning over, Charles frantically unfastened the Messenger's seat straps. One of the attendants helped him out of the seat and down to the runway. Placing the relaxed Messenger's arm around his neck, Charles and the attendant rushed him down the flight of stairs to the elevator. In a few minutes, they entered the first-floor emergency room. A woman ran up behind Charles calling out to him, "I have a Raymond Rogers on the line for a…Mr. Charles Kelly. Mr. Kelly?" Charles never even looked back at her as he rushed along with the attendant, the Messenger past the numerous persons in the room. There were several severely injured people sitting or leaning over in chairs, propped up against the walls, or lining the floor. A young intern with a clipboard in his hand was preparing the waiting ailing people in what seemed like a random.

Messenger's eyes flooded with a degree of pain. He watched a mother comfort her school-age child who had an abnormally swollen foot.

Charles rushed over to the emergency desk and stepped in his hurry to the front of the line.

"Miss, I need some help here. I have a severely injured man who needs medical attention right away. I don't have time to go through all the procedures."

He reached into his pocket and pulled out his wallet.

"Here's my driver's license, station I.D., and insurance card. Please…"

The receptionist was a young woman with an overly teased blond hairdo, and a pink sweater tied around her neck and draped over her shoulders. She was smoking a nervous cigarette and had a transistor radio on her desk turned up the too high volume.

"Do you have any credentials for your friend?" the receptionist asked blandly.

"I have credentials. He's hurt. Isn't this a hospital?" Charles angrily snapped.

"Excuse me, sir, we have special procedures for hardship cases."

She placed several foundation forms over the counter.

"You can appeal to any of these charity foundations. Just make your selections and call the numbers. If you explain your case adequately, I'm sure something can be arranged."

"What?" Charles shrieked in disbelief. "What if he were dying? Who has that much time?"

"Listen, sir," the receptionist retorted. "There are several cases ahead of you, so would you please step aside?"

"But I need help!" Charles demanded.

The receptionist turned away from Charles and pointed to two guards standing at the edge of the hall.

"Security."

She waved her finger and the guards came up to the desk quickly.

"You have a problem, Angel?" one of the guards asked.

"Alright! Alright," Charles cut in. "Listen. My wife works here…Ann Kelly. She's the head nurse on the ninth floor. Will you dial her extension for me? And let me talk to her, please?"

The receptionist looked at Charles's identification again just as one of the security guards grabbed his arm. She looked back up at Charles.

"Ann is your wife, huh?"

"Yes, ninth floor. Call her for me, will you, please?"

The receptionist distrustfully glanced at the identification again and decided to give Charles the benefit of the doubt. She waved the security guards away.

"Okay. But stand over there," the receptionist pointed, "until I get her."

Charles stepped away from the desk and looked in the direction he'd left the Messenger. He wasn't there. A jolt of fear shot through him as he turned around in every direction searching for the missing visitor. Hidden behind a huddled group of injured, he saw stooped down, the Messenger, tenderly consoling the mother and tending to the child with the swollen foot.

He quickly paced over beside him.

"Ah," Charles stammered, not knowing quite what to call him.

Turning around but not getting up, the Messenger searched him over, neither offering expectance nor rejecting his beckoning. Not being able to interpret the look on the stranger's face, Charles stood there, frozen.

"Ah, Mr. Kelly," came the voice from the reception desk. "I have your wife on the line."

Keeping his eyes on the Messenger who had returned to tending the mother and child, Charlie walked over to the desk and took the phone from the receptionist.

"Ann. Come to the first-floor emergency room. I need your help to get a friend admitted into the hospital. Please hurry. I think he needs help, but he doesn't seem to realize it."

"What's wrong? What's the problem, darling?" Ann nervously asked not knowing what to make of it.

"I don't have time to explain now," Charles said. "Just come right away."

"Alright. I'm on my way."

Ann dropped the phone on the receiver and ran straight for the elevators.

"Nurse Kelly," one of the aides called out to her. "Doctor Willis is expecting you in the south wing."

Ann pressed the buttons on the elevators, "Tell him I'm busy. An emergency. Get someone else."

Charles went over to the Messenger and gently lifted his arm. The Messenger offered no resistance and was guided over to clear space by the door. Taking off his jacket, Charles laid it on the floor against the wall. The Messenger sat on the floor against the jacket. Charles then began to pace between the two entrances, waiting for his wife to arrive.

When Ann exhaustedly entered the room, Charles walked directly over to her.

"What's wrong What happened? Where is this friend you're talking about?"

"It's a long story. Please, Ann, don't ask any questions. Listen to me." Charles put his hands on her shoulder and looked into her eyes.

"You see that bearded man next to the wall?" Charles nodded his head in the stranger's direction. "Well, something happened."

He then began to choke up. Tears streamed from his eyes as he looked at the ceiling in an effort to collect himself.

Ann became even more concerned when she saw his emotional stat. "What is it, Charles? Tell me."

"I…I can't get it out just now. Not here," Charles chocked. "But after he's admitted, and we get some time I'll tell you everything. Ann. Please. Get him admitted."

Turning away, Ann went over to the receptionist's desk.

"Miss Miller, that man against the wall, call an orderly for a wheelchair and get a bed ready for him."

"I'm sorry Nurse Kelly, but that man has no identification or proper insurance plan. I cannot authorize any movement until he's been cleared. I'll have to…"

"I'll take full responsibility," Ann said sharply.

"Yes, ma'am."

The receptionist, annoyed by Ann's tone, reluctantly obeyed.

Ann then walked over to the Messenger with Charles beside her. She reached down, took his wrist, and looked at her watch.

"What's your friend's name?" she asked.

Charles looked down at the Messenger who was gazing forward.

"Ah…his name? Charles Kelly," came his reply.

Ann definitely did not understand but willingly went along with the whole thing.

An orderly came in with a wheelchair, and Ann signaled him in her direction.

"Would you put that gentleman," Ann pointed to the Messenger. "In this chair and move him to…" She quickly stepped over to the reception desk and read the allocation sheet. "Bed says on the fifth floor, uhh…make it five-forty."

With Charles's assistance, the orderly helped the Messenger onto the chair while Ann went back to the receptionist's desk. She went into the admission files and pulled out a form filling the necessary proper information.

"Now, run this through the terminal," Ann requested, handing the receptionist the forms. Picking up the phone, Ann dialed an associate on the fifth floor. She knew of a space opened for a retired banker, but she had him bumped knowing his illness was not serious. She then called an intern she had become familiar with. He was resting in the main lounge but agreed to examine the Messenger when he was processed.

Charles was standing by the door with his arms folded, staring blankly down the hall. He was filled with compassion for the strange visitor whose name he didn't even know. He was overawed by the supernatural way the Messenger had transpired.

Ann walked over to Charles and placed her arm around his waist in an effort to calm him.

"Ann," Charles said, still shaken by what was occurring. "Is there someplace we can be alone? Someplace where we can talk."

Ann looked at her watch, "It's two o'clock. Between shifts. The nurse's lounge should be empty about now. Why don't we go there?"

The couple headed toward the elevator. Charles was silent, collecting his thoughts to explain the questions he knew Ann was sure to have. He struggled to think of a way to describe the appearance of the Messenger. They got to the third floor and walked down the hallway to a nicely furnished room with vending machines along one wall. Going to a corner of the room, Charles sat down on a brightly colored vinyl couch while Ann got two cups of coffee from one of the machines. She then sat down next to Charles, angling her knees against his as she handed him a cup.

"Who was that man, Charles?" she asked.

Charles took a sip of coffee.

"I…I don't know. It's all so totally unbelievable."

Ann was trying to take in what Charles was saying, but he seemed so incoherent.

"Slow down, Charles," she said, "now tell me to step by step what happened."

Charles took another sip before beginning.

"I was sent on assignment, flying over Mirage Lake when, all of a sudden, the chopper stopped cold."

"What?" Ann gasped.

Charles began to shudder at the thought of it.

"I couldn't move. I was pinned down in my seat like a rag doll. The instruments were going haywire. The sky got dark, a very chilling dark. I was frightened out of my wits. Then out of nowhere, this bolt of lightning hit the ground, and as quickly as it started, it was over."

Ann's fear became more intense. She gripped Charles's arm and began searching him over.

"Are you alright? How badly did…?"

"I'm okay," Charles cut in. "I pulled the chopper under control. But what I saw was the most terrifying and unforgettable thing I have ever seen."

Choking up, Charles put his head down. Ann put her hand on the back of his neck and massaged it lightly, urging Charles.

"Down there where the lighting had struck…" Charles continued, "down on the ground…I saw a man."

The impact of what Charles had said hit Ann all at once. She sat up and put her hand over her mouth. Her eyes widened, and her realization turned to shock.

"You…You mean…"

She was afraid to say it.

"Yes, Ann," Charles confirmed. "That was him."

"Maybe he was already there." Ann offered, fighting to disbelieve what Charles was saying. "Maybe he was there and got struck by the lightning."

"Ann!" Charles called, trying to get her to focus on him, "Ann! Listen to me. He was not there before. There was nobody there before."

They both sat silent for a moment. Ann took a sip of her coffee and tried to settle down. She placed her hand over Charles.

"Did he speak?" she asked.

"He said a few things. Some of them I didn't quite understand. He said something about his being a Messenger."

"Well, let us go talk to him now," Ann said. "Perhaps he will tell us what this all means."

"Let's let him rest now," Charles said, standing up. "I think there'll be time to find out. Whatever it is, I think it is a pivotal point to all of the other things that have been happening. This could be the chance we've been expecting for so long."

Ann stood up and hugged Charles around his waist, burying her head in his chest, "You know, I should feel even more afraid Charles, but for some reason, I feel relieved. Whatever it is, I feel God is on our side."

The embrace lasted a few extra moments, the couple not wanting to part, but Ann still had people depending on her, and Charles had to get the chopper back to base.

"What are you going to tell Rogers?" Ann asked as they approached the door.

"I haven't decided," Charles replied. "He won't be happy, but I can't concern myself with that now. I'll try to be home early tonight."

They kissed at the door one last time before they parted.

In the medium-sized room, a young black intern stood over the relaxed Messenger and landed a pleasant bedside manner.

"Good afternoon Mr. Kelly," the intern greeted. "How are you feeling?"

"Everything is in divine order," the Messenger replied.

The intern unwrapped the bandaged wounds and started to examine them before washing. They were odd wounds, unlike anybody had seen. They resembled puncture marks, yet the ends of the holes were normally formed. It seemed that the holes were a part of this patient's normal physiology. But if that were the case, why had they been bleeding? He washed the hands and examined them again.

"How long have you had these injuries? Where did you receive them?" the intern asked in genuine amazement.

"He was perceived as a criminal, yet he committed no crime. I want to be like him," the Messenger answered.

The young intern frowned inquisitively and turned to get new wrappings, "You speak strangely too," he murmured while he wrapped the Messenger's hands with clean bandages.

The intern then took out a blood pressure meter and put the constriction strap around the Messenger's arm. He pumped up the pressure and read the mercury which was fixed like an iron bar on twelve over eight. It never fluctuated even for an instant, and it didn't appear to float to that level. The phenomenon was so unbelievable that the intern tapped the glass tube trying to get the gauge to move. It wouldn't. The same thing happened with the thermometer. He checked the Messenger's heart rate, which was also regular.

The intern stood away from his patient, amazed. He hurriedly pulled a measurement device from his bag of equipment. Upon measuring the Messenger's hands and feet, he found him to be anatomically perfect from left to right. Neither toe nor finger as in any way different from its opposite.

"I've never seen anything like this," he stammered. "There's nothing wrong with you Mr. Kelly, but I think we might keep you here a day or so for observation. You have a very unusual physiology."

The Messenger said nothing but lay there, meditating in peace. The intern nervously repacked his bag and placed the loose paper and odd wrapping in the trash basket.

"We'll have a specialist look you over early tomorrow morning or even later this evening if we can arrange it. In the meantime, you get some rest." The intern took another questioning glance at the Messenger and then left the room. A nurse came in immediately afterward and pulled the privacy partition around him.

It was later in the evening, Ann's regular time to get off work. There had been an emergency when another head nurse had fainted from dizzy spells and Ann had to cover for the ailing woman. She had to pull two duties in one shift and the overlap held her longer than she had expected. Surely, Charles was home by now and Linda's teacher must be anxiously awaiting her arrival, Ann had been so busy she hadn't had time to check on the unexpected visitor. She struggled to piece together the events Charles had described. His story was frantic. It is seen totally unreal and yet the feelings she'd sensed all that day indeed even as he told her were frighteningly real.

The Spyder pulled into the emptied driveway of the school. Ann parked on the side of the building, got out and entered the main entrance. As she walked down the hallway, her footsteps echoed against the walls. She came upon Linda's classroom and saw that Mrs. Wilson got out and entered the walls. She came upon Linda's classroom and saw Mrs. Wilson talking to the vice principal sitting on the edge of her desk.

Linda saw her mother and rose up to go toward the door. As Mrs. Wilson noticed Linda's reaction, she turned to see Ann standing in the doorway.

"Mrs. Kellys, how are you? I trust everything is alright," the teacher greeted.

"Oh, things are fine. I was held over a little longer at work today. One of the girls took ill."

Ann's somewhat nervous demeanor struck the teacher oddly. The vice principal looked around and lowered his glasses to get a peek at Ann.

"Mrs. Kelly," he said, "Fine young girl you have."

"Thank you," Ann said graciously.

Linda came over to Ann with her books and they abruptly turned to leave.

"Thank you, Mrs. Wilson," Ann said, looking back. "Nice to see you again Mr. Hunter."

As Mr. Hunter heard the shallow footsteps down the hall, he looked over at the middle-aged teacher.

"What was that all about?"

"I have no idea," Mrs. Wilson answered shifting over to her desk. "The little girl, Linda, has been acting very strangely. She's been behaving in a listless manner. For the past few weeks. I thought that the extra attention we've been centering on her would make a difference, but it hasn't seemed to."

The vice principal hummed quizzically and put his finger over his mouth, tapping it thoughtfully.

"She's a clone, isn't she? Do you think that may have anything to do with it?"

"I don't know," Mrs. Wilson answered. "We've had other clones here. Not very many, but enough to have observed certain patterns. And I don't see anything right now I can put my finger on."

"Maybe it's her family," Mr. Hunter interjected. "I understand they are, well kind of…overly religious. Possibly that overemphasis on religion might be making the girl neurotic."

"Yes, the mother, Mrs. Kellys, was behaving rather imbalanced today as you saw. I understand that sometimes emotional instability tends to run among the church type," Mrs. Wilson added.

She then leaned over and reached into a lower drawer in her desk. She brought out many pencils and popsicle sticks tied together with rubber bands.

"Look at these," she said, handing the vice principal some of the crosses. "Linda had been tying these sticks together and giving them to people, teachers, classmates, bus drivers just anybody, for the past week."

"I'm no expert, but it does suggest a certain compulsion," Mr. Hunter suggested as he took one of the crosses and studied it. "A fixation on the cross. The symbol of Christianity. She's quite young to be displaying such an intense attitude for something like this. At her age, she should be dipping in ink wells and swapping boyfriends. Something is definitely unhealthy about this."

"Then you think it is most likely the parents?" the teacher asked in earnest. "Things certainly seem to suggest that; it is more than likely the case. I think I'll talk to Mayers about this. He may find a reason to call in a professional to sit down with that family."

"It would be for the girls' own good," Mrs. Wilson said.

She then stood up and breathed in a sigh.

"Well, now that's taken care of, and everything is done; I think I'll go home and put my feet up. I've already made Philip's dinner, so he'll do nothing but watch the game all night."

She shifted her eyes to the side, hoping the vice principal caught the longing tone in her voice.

"I'm not doing anything special tonight," Mr. Hunter returned, "and my wife's out of town. What say we have a drink this evening before you make it in?"

Mrs. Wilson's heart leaped as the hint got across.

"I'm buying," she said as she reached for her briefcase under the desk.

Mr. Hunter placed his hand over hers and stroked it. He took the briefcase from her.

"No. Tonight's my treat."

Chapter 10

The Messenger's Way

The visitor calmly laid in his bed with his hands clasped upon his chest, meditating. The curtain partition separated him from his roommate.

To the right of the Messenger's bed, a very wealthy businessman lay in minor pain, puffing on a cigar and loudly talking to three friends.

John Spaulding, a sixty-three-year-old industrialist with a flabby chin line and grayish head of hair, was the loudest of the four. His bedside tabletop was littered with flowers, get well cards, and various wrapped bottles of alcohol denoting the numerous contacts and acquaintances fond of him.

"Listen, fellows. Pour up some of that Black Label there. My first secretary gave me that. Good twenty-year-old scotch."

Spaulding had been a hard worker and a heavy drinker as well as a driving businessman.

"We'll toast up, John," said one of his partners. "But I don't think you should have anymore. I doubt you're even supposed to be drinking."

"Nonsense, nonsense, if I wasn't supposed to be drinking, I'd be dead already."

Spaulding began to laugh and cough at the same time at the joke, but he grimaced in pain when he felt the twinge of pain in his stomach.

"You sound pretty bad. I think we better leave," another offered.

John kept coughing and waving the hand with the cigar in it.

"Ridiculous. You boys don't have to go anywhere. There's nothing wrong with me. They'll cut this thing out of me tomorrow, and I'll be back out on the golf course by Friday."

"Sure, that's right," his friend consoled.

Another broke out four short paper cups and poured the Black Label.

"To the golf course."

He raised his cup.

"To the golf course," they all responded.

They then quickly turned up the drinks, John looking particularly pained as his drink went down.

There was then a moment of uneasy silence. A visitor of John slid the movable solid screened partition along with the runner and peered over at the Messenger lying calmly.

"Ah!" he said, sarcastically. "Get a load of this. A hippie!"

Spaulding turned over on his side and chuckled. "A hippie? I thought those went out with high button shoes and the buggy whip."

"Hey, hippie," one of the men called over. "How about a shot of this stuff?" He rolled the liquid around in the cup while he looked at the Messenger. "It'll put hair on your chest!"

The four of them broke up laughing at the joke. John Spaulding laughed piercingly loud and then chortled into a broken cough which grew more painful with each heave. His company was still laughing not knowing as he leaned over the side of the bed, the pain hacking his stomach with each involuntary spasm. He honked a strained miserable heave, and as he raised up his eyes, met the Messenger. There was temporary hesitation as the sick man broke the glance and sat up in the bed.

"He doesn't want any of this," a visitor interjected. "They only like drugs. Maybe we can send him up a pusher on the way out."

The three others broke out in laughter again, this time, they were not joined by John.

"Hand me that bottle," he said.

The visitors stopped and searched each other over.

"John, you shouldn't be drinking this much," one said. "I mean; a lot of medication is probably already in your system. Liquor might not do you too much good. A drink is minor but the whole bottle?"

"Yeah, John," another added. "You know how you can get."

"I don't need anybody telling me what I can and cannot drink!" John screamed. "There is nothing wrong with me! I feel fine. Just a little upset stomach. A little cyst. No big deal. I'll be out of here by Friday."

"Now hand me that bottle. Do you boys think you're talking to a kid? I know what I'm doing! Hand it to me!"

One of his acquaintances reluctantly handed John the bottle of Black Label, and he took it almost in defiance. He glanced defensively at his visitors and then turned the bottle upward, taking a few swallows. The pain he felt was obvious as he winced after the drink. He then put the bottle on the floor next to the bed and placed his now burnt-out cigar in a nearby ashtray.

"John, we gotta be going," a friend said as they all readied themselves for departure.

"Aww, come on guys, stay for a few more drinks."

John seemed genuinely disappointed.

"Wish we could, John, but we gotta go. Big day tomorrow."

They were already filing out.

"Take it easy," one said.

"Stay away from those nurses," another commented.

The three strolled out of the room and down the hall to the elevators.

The Messenger lay silent on his bed as he heard the very pained coughs of John Spaulding on the other side of the partition which had not been completely closed. He turned his head and saw John put the bottle up to his mouth and struggle down another swallow of the scotch. Some of the light brown liquid rolled down the side of Mr. Spaulding's mouth and onto the linen beneath him. He wiped his mouth with his forearm and another cough caught him, doubling him over.

After gaining some composure, the pain still sharp in his stomach, the ailing businessman caught the Messenger's eyes.

"Ah!" he called out aggressively, "You! Hippie! What's your name?"

The Messenger remained silent. He returned to his prior position, gazing at the ceiling.

"You want a shot of this?"

There wasn't an answer.

"I'm talking to you, Hippie! Don't ignore me. I offered you a shot of my fine booze. This isn't cheap stuff. I drink the best in the world. Even a drug popping hippie can appreciate the taste of something smooth."

The Messenger then turned over on his side and raised up on his elbow in a comfortable position. There was a searing look in his eyes but soft compassion in his demeanor.

"What time do you have?" he asked.

Spaulding was caught off guard by the soft clear question asked by the stranger. He thought his own statements were antagonizing, yet the Messenger was totally unmoved.

"Uh…time…uh…" Spaulding stuttered. "It's…uh…"

He peeped down at this watch.

"It's uh, eight-fifteen."

"You are wise in the ways of this world," the Messenger responded. "By your teaching, you know the time of day. But by your actions, you cannot read the signs of the time."

"What are you? High on grass?" the sarcastic John Spaulding shot back.

"Were I in any such state, your wisdom of the ways of this world would reveal the truth to you, for it is faithful. And yet you perceive there is no such fault in me. You know I am not. It is your own anguish that has said so."

The direct, firm words rang in Spaulding's ears, unlike any others he had heard. Fighting to gain control, John sat the bottle on the table next to him and took a good look at the Messenger.

"Who are you?" he asked.

"It matters not my identity but yours. You are at a crossroads. Who you have been, and who you must decide to be? Your future rests on your decision. I ask you now, do you know who you are?"

John was puzzled at the question, "You speak to me in riddles."

He then felt the sharp pain in his stomach throb.

"Do you know yourself?" the Messenger persisted.

"Of course, I do!" John squeezed out between the pains.

"Then that side of you. That sinful side. John the unforgiving, John the mocker, John the arrogant, that John must part. It is that John who has pained you so much. It is that John which has brought you here."

Spaulding listened intently. Something about what the Messenger was saying was getting through to him. He coughed again in anguish, and a hint of bitterness came over him.

"What do you mean?" he choked out, almost in defiance. "I'm proud of myself. I'm rich, I'm successful. I like me the way I am."

"So, you say," the Messenger replied. "Let every man be right in his own eyes. That the whole world might see him and envy him, that he might show the world one face and hide another."

The Messenger then gazed into the pained eyes of the sick man.

"Here you lie. So, you say; satisfied to be who you are. But you do not want to be here."

The resistance in John Spaulding began to break down. He grabbed at the pain in his stomach and doubled over. An awful piercing cry screeched from his throat. Tears started to stream from his eyes. The ailing man began to weep uncontrollably.

"I'm sick!" he grunted between gasps.

"You cannot heal yourself. Your life is not your own. Release that part of you John. Let the life that is yet in you be full."

The Messenger felt the pain of John and pleaded with him.

"Let go! Let go!" John complained. "You tell me to let go. You talk in riddles. If you know so much; do more than talk. Make this pain stop. Make it go away!"

The Messenger's eyes saddened. He laid back again and focused upward.

"Yeah," came the ailing man's response. "I didn't think you could."

Spaulding then roughly took the bottle off the nightstand. He gulped a few swigs and relaxed on his side. After a series of spasmatic coughs, the sickened patient dozed off, still feeling the sharp throbbing pains.

The Messenger reclined solemnly in the night. He pondered his desk, and he meditated on the goodness of God. He thought about the days of Christ and of the days of Christ's passages. The words, the ways, were true now and forever. As they were:

Then, certain of the scribes and the Pharisees answered, saying, Master, we would see a sign from thee.

But he answered and said unto them. An evil and adulterous generation seeketh after a sign; and there shall no sign be given to it, but the sign of Jonah and prophet Jonah: For as Jonah was three days and three nights in the whale's belly, so shall the son of man be three days and three nights in the heart of the earth.

The man of Nineveh shall rise in judgment with this generation, and shall condemn it: because they repented at the teaching of Jonah; and behold, a greater than Jonah is here.

When the unclear spirit is gone out of a man, he walketh through dry places, seeking rest, and findeth none.

Then he saith, I will return into my house from whence I came out; and when he has come, he findeth it empty, swept and garnished.

Then goeth he, and taketh with himself seven other spirits more wicked than himself, and they enter in and dwell there: and the last state of that man is worse than the first. Even so, shall it be also unto this wicked generation?

The late-night introspection of the Messenger was interrupted by the moans of John Spaulding. Sitting up on the side of the bed, the Messenger stepped into his sandals on the floor and slid the cloth divider completely aside. He gazed at Spaulding and found the ailing man holding his pillow to his stomach, rocking back and forth, blurting out low sobs.

"I don't want to die. Oh, God. Please help me. I'm still young, please don't let me die."

The Messenger leaned over, and as John sensed presence; he caught sight of him.

"What are you doing near me, hippie?" John said in anger. "You can't help me. Get away from me."

"Why do you weep, John? Do you now know that every second you breathe is life? Why do you wail the cry of death? Your breath."

"Get away from me, you riddle-talking hippie," John demanded. "Talk is cheap. Why are you bothering me? Let me die in peace."

"Do you pray?" the Messenger asked.

"Pray?" John asked again, annoyed by the stranger's conversation. "Why should I pray. You said it yourself; I'm a prideful, selfish man."

"Look at yourself, John."

"Look at wh—" John tried to counter, but the Messenger gently cut in.

"Reflect on John. Not with eyes of self-pity, but with eyes of truth. Mirror down inside yourself. Down where only John can see. No one but you and God. You've lived for many years. You've done so much."

John Spaulding continued to absorb pain from the inside. This time it seemed not as much from cancer as from his own inner discontent.

The Messenger clasped John's hand.

"Do you see yourself?"

Eyes closed tightly, John Spaulding began to nod.

"I would like that the whole man change," the Messenger said, staring intently at John.

"Would you change? To start life a fresh, anew. Will you change?"

Spaulding's eyes began to tighten, and tears formed in their corners.

"I want to," he mumbled slowly, whispering.

"Then you must," the Messenger intoned. "You must change. Reject all darkness that is within you. It will flee from you. Confess. Pray. Say what is in your heart."

A low muffled whine came from John's throat, followed by a loud shrieking grunt. With a grip on John's hand, the Messenger held his own other palm, angled upwards in a sublime gesture.

"Do you feel?" the Messenger asked in a lower tone than he'd talked before.

"Yes," came the weeping cry from John.

"Then accept him. Let him change you; my Master. You will never be the same."

The Messenger released John's hand. Rolling over on his side, the ailing man buried his head in the pillow. The Messenger then looked out the large picture window between the two beds. The moonlight showed brightly and cast its soft light over the sick man's bed. The stranger stepped back out of the rays of light and motioned his hand in the glow, casting a shadow over the ailing man's entire abdomen.

"Some are ill because they are ill. Others are because they wish it so. As John has chosen. Let it be."

The moans from the bed opposite the Messenger's grew less frequent until John Spaulding slipped into a restful sleep.

At five forty-five the next morning, a slender middle-aged nurse came into the room with two orderlies who pushed a light rolling bed. The moved swiftly and professionally to John's Spaulding's side. Checking her chart again, she aroused the patient gently.

"Wake up, Mr. Spaulding. Time to get prepped for the anesthesiologist."

The patient groggily rolled over and rubbed his eyes. The experienced nurse observed the near-empty scotch bottle on the floor by the nightstand. She pointed the mischief out to the attendants.

"You're going to need a doliar-pattern and a flush out after what you've had, Mr. Spaulding," she said, nodding at the bottle.

"Put him on transport," the nurse told the orderlies.

"Where am I going?" Spaulding inquired, still with cobwebs in his head.

"Surgery preparation," the nurse answered. "We're going to get you ready for the operation. You're scheduled for seven o'clock. Don't worry; you've got Dr. Gullicson. He's our best."

"Can't I see my wife?" Spaulding asked.

"Your family and friends are downstairs in the waiting room. After your recovery period, they will be allowed upstairs," the nurse answered cheerfully but firmly.

John Spaulding relaxed peacefully on the bed and was rolled out of the room. He closed his eyes for a few minutes. Soon, John found himself in a brightly lit room that had a strange yellow glow about it. He was told to disrobe and recline inside of a large oval-shaped machine. The machine was set on a three-foot big platform that resembled a conveyor. Soon, the surgery-prep technician came into the room from behind the glass-encased area for sensory monitoring. He connected an assortment of wires to John's body. The technician then put plastic shields over John's eyes. Upon returning to the observation booth, he switched different colors of intense light inside the contained area. Johns was then given a pill to swallow and contained on through another hour of preparations. When the surgery time grew nearer, he was given a green backless paper gown and placed in a sterile white room for waiting. Not much time passed before he was wheeled into the operating room.

The instance he was placed on the padded operating table, the information of his vital signs appeared on large screens to be monitored, above the patient. Each screen gave actual diagrams and outlines of different organs and vital signs. Every instant at different intervals, an organ would appear and a line lighted diagram of its various angles couples with a moment-by-moment reaction would write themselves, computerized next to the diagram.

The masked anesthesiologist cupped a plastic breathing mask over John's nose and mouth. John only momentarily saw the medical team as he faded quickly, his vital signs functioning normally.

The intense studious elderly head surgeon maneuvered around and inside Mr. Spaulding's abdomen like a fine pointer on a delicate subject. He gave precise instructions to his team and clearly orchestrated the operation like a master.

In moments, the surgeon got to his point of attack. As he examined the area of the intestine in question, a serious frown came over his face.

"Ah, nurse," he called out nervously. "Scan that for me."

The nurse quickly picked up a short tube-shaped sensor and held it six inches from the exposed incision.

"Uniform doctor," she reported. "No excess heat."

"There has to be a mistake," the main assistant said in surprise. "I examined this man myself yesterday morning."

The assistant grabbed the sensor from the nurse. He held it over the injured area, but the reading was the same. He then angrily walked around to the other side of the table while the others watched in question. He pressed an entry into the terminal mount for a specific organ check on-screen number four. The computer registered a large detailed blow-up of the intestine on the screen. They all showed up normal.

"There isn't any cancer in this man," the head surgeon finally said. He snapped off his rubber gloves, "Nurse, close up for me, will you?"

The head nurse of the team promptly began procedures while the head surgeon stormed out of the operating room. The taller younger assistant followed closely behind.

"I swear to you, Karl; that man had cancer. Yesterday, he was in a lot of pain. I gave him a sedative myself."

The older doctor turned and glared squarely at the subordinate, "Listen, Mister. I don't know what kind of joke this was supposed to be, but I am a competent physician. My time is very valuable to me. Each minute I waste is time I could use pursuing other important matters. I consider your diagnosis highly irresponsible and you can bet you're going to get a full write up about this fiasco!"

The angered doctor then turned and whisked through the swinging doors en route to the dressing room. The assistant stood there, hurt and puzzled. He anguished in his mind to figure out what had gone wrong. At first, he questioned his medical knowledge, but he had been too sure of the diagnosis to be wrong.

Walking back into the operating room, the assistant raised up his surgical mask. The nurse was just finishing up the closing.

"Nurse!" he demanded another of his team. "I want full micro discs of this whole operation. I want every record on Spaulding's case from the day he entered the hospital door to the last stitch he gets!"

The orderly assistants placed him on a transport bed and carted him away to the recovery room where John Spaulding lay under the heavy effect of the drugs for an hour and a half.

At around two o'clock, the patient groggily started to come to. He fought to focus on the mirror on the wall in a corner of the room, but his consciousness kept slipping. Eventually, Mr. Spaulding was able to control his vision. He looked around the room and was able to focus on a table and desk on the far side. He wanted to sit up, but his mind reacted to the sharp pains he'd been getting whenever he did so too quickly. So, John Spaulding sat up slowly and placed his hand over his stomach. He tensed, expecting to feel the pain that had been with him so long, but he surprisingly felt nothing. John was free; free from the torment cancer had caused him.

He eased back down and thought about the events that had happened last night. That strange man had made him see himself as he never had before. He felt he'd made some kind of commitment to God. His heart felt lighter. The burdens were gone.

John enjoyed the worry-free feeling almost as much as he did the lack of pain. But somehow, he still doubted. He lay there trying to reconstruct the events of the previous night. He recalled asking the Messenger to stop the pain.

"There," he whispered to himself.

It had merely been a lot of talks. Even though emotionally he felt better, freer; it had been the doctors. The men of knowledge did the real work. Yes, that was it! Perhaps through his own drained weakness that weird hippie had talked him into or out of himself.

John felt his abdomen again. The pain was gone. The doctors had done their work. He felt terrific, and he probably would be out on the golf course by at least next week. Men of learning. Men of medicine. When you need them, he thought; a doctor could be a man's best friend.

As he was amusing himself in thought, a nurse came in with a thermometer and a blood pressure meter.

"How do you feel, Mr. Spaulding?" the nurse asked.

"Excellent!" John replied.

"Boy, your people sure did a great job on my pain. I can hardly feel a thing." John pressed his hand over his stomach.

The nurse pulled his hand away and set it on his chest.

"You'll loosen your bandage," she smiled.

After checking him over, the nurse called in a young candy stripper to assist an orderly in carting Mr. Spaulding to his room. John joked cheerfully with people in the hallway as he was rolled on to an elevator.

There was a young intern there recording information on his bed chart when the cart with Mr. Spaulding came in. the intern helped the two put John back into his bed.

"Is he coming from the recovery room?" the intern asked.

"Yes, John is quite spry for a man who just came out of surgery," the candy stripper remarked, while patting the patient on the leg.

"How do you feel, Mr. Spaulding?" the young intern asked.

"Tremendous," John replied. "I'll send whoever operated on me a box of my finest cigars!"

A mildly disturbing look flashed on the intern's face. He glanced at the candy stripper in question.

"You mean he doesn't know?"

"Uh. No, not exactly," the young lady answered. "Nobody's had time to tell him."

"What? Know what? What hasn't anybody had time to tell me?" John inquired.

The intern rechecked his chart and then seriously addressed John, "There was no cancerous growth. All of our readings in the operating room were negative. Regardless of the prognosis when you came in here, by the time you got to the operating room…it just wasn't there."

Spaulding's first reaction was anger, "You mean you people cut on me when nothing was there? What do you mean no cancer? This is an…"

As he bellowed in anger, John Spaulding turned and noticed the empty bed beside him. Then suddenly, he recalled the words of the Messenger from the night before.

"Ah! Oh my God!" the businessman shouted.

He strained, pointing his finger at the empty bed that once held the Messenger.

"It was him! It was him!" the patient shouted ecstatically as a nurse grabbed hold of one of his arms. She tried to calm him down.

"Praise God! Oh my God, thank you! Thank you! It was him! It was him!"

The intern ran around the side of the bed and grabbed the other arm. He motioned for the candy stripper who ran out of the room.

"It was him! Oh, thank you, Lord! Thank you!"

John Spaulding was fighting the nurse and the intern as he shook the bed in vibrant jubilation.

"My God, without a doubt I believe you, thank you! Thank you!"

The young girl came back with a kit from the hall desk and quickly gave it to the intern. He clumsily unwrapped a needle and fumbled through the preparation of a sedative. After pulling the needle down with his teeth, he shot John in the arm, and after a bit more of an exciting struggle, the jubilant patient succumbed.

Chapter 11
Days of Passage

The Messenger had left the hospital and wandered into the streets of Los Angeles to survey a world that had lost its grip. As he walked along the sidewalk men and women propositioned him and a few of the bolder homosexuals attempted to touch him, but he shunned mildly but firmly their advances.

He took in the spoil and devastation of the tenements and burned out businesses. As he walked down one particularly devastated block, a man in a long coat held it open, accosting him about buying stolen items. A group of youths with letters and symbols of street gang emblems sewn to the backs of their jackets chased one lone youth who was running furiously just ahead of them. The young boy, terror in his eyes, ran past the Messenger and up to the side of a boarded-up walkway where a building once stood. He frantically scurried over the makeshift boarded fence and disappeared across the brick strewn lot. An instant past, the young toughs in the gang jackets shot past the Messenger, the last one trailing a bicycle chain with a lock on the end of it wrapped around his fist.

It was not hard to believe the state that the world seemed to be in for the Messenger was prepared for his mission. How he felt had no bearing on what he was to witness. He only knew what must be, and his part in a greater whole.

Looking up at the windows above, the Messenger could see an old fat woman with rollers in her hair sitting aimlessly, staring out of the window. A little further down he saw an older unemployed man in an undershirt also gazing emptily outward. He looked to another rooftop as he walked and saw two children who couldn't have been any more than five or six scooting out dangerously on a ledge trying to catch a pigeon.

As he was looking up, his attention was shifted by a cursing shouting match at the corner by two rather tattered winos who were arguing ferociously over some pennies pitched at the cracks in the sidewalk. One, more aggressive than the other, began to boast himself up while pointing his finger in the other one's face. After a few moments of this, the shorter one put his head down and plowed into the pointing wino's stomach, knocking him to the ground. The two of them tussled there on the side-walk while the others, who had been sitting around talking and trading bottles, didn't seem moved by the event.

For hours, the Messenger wandered through the streets of Los Angeles. The taking in of all the events, the sights and sounds, the cries of despair, the hunger, the misery, he took it all in with pain in his eyes and hurt in his heart for this state of humanity. Truly, this was not how men were meant to be. It seemed all of what he observed led men toward their own destruction. And yet, he knew and would not stray from the message that he must bear. That, until the last step of the walk of his third day would not be fulfilled.

After he had observed as much as he would; an inner perception told him to stop in the block where he was. He slowly stood, acknowledging his surroundings and studying his perception. At the far corner of the block, he saw some over-dressed women standing in a doorway. Across the street, on an opposite corner, he saw a crippled man with a cup filled with pencils sipping on a bottle wrapped in a brown paper bag. Toward the middle of the block, the Messenger saw some old packing crates which were obviously used for sitting. He walked over to the crates and took a seat calmly there.

His eyes relaxed as he studied the dingy, grayish old structures across the street. The doorways seemed as if they were huddled together and even though there were tenants living inside, they somehow looked abandoned.

"Move and you're dead!"

A voice came from the left side of the Messenger. He shifted his eyes lightly and saw a knife's blade pointed directly at his neck.

The aggressor, a short young man of medium build, wearing a green tattered military jacket with an unshaven face with fierce in his accosting. He expected the same feared reaction he usually got.

The Messenger said nothing and became even calmer under this threat. The mugger couldn't see any noticeable change in the Messenger's movements but he somehow detected the calm mood which took him off guard.

"Alright! Give it up!" The aggressor snapped his fingers, demanding money or other valuables.

"I give to you all that I have," the Messenger said with great compassion in his voice. He then turned his head and looked up at his attacker. "But I have nothing."

The aggressor would have normally forced the blade further on the assailant for turning his head and not obeying his orders, but as he stared into the Messenger's face; it almost seemed like he lost his will. He even felt himself a little bit frightened of this strange figure.

"I am much like you," the gentle voice added. "I am searching for something of value."

The mugger began to tighten his grip on the blade in an attempt to get himself back in control of the situation.

"Listen, sucker! I got no time for games. Now come up with something and do it quicker, or I'll spill you on this sidewalk."

The Messenger continued to study the face of his attacker. His searching showed genuine kindness and understanding. There was a reaching out in his eyes that threw the aggressor off balance. In a very deliberate but slow, continuous motion, the Messenger cut his hand over the blade part of the knife. He smiled warmly, lifting the knife gently out of the mugger's hand. The mugger was so shocked by the action; he could not move.

"The cutting edge of our inner pain. I wish I had enough for you. But look at me. I am but a poor man."

The Messenger then placed the knife down at his side, searching himself. He looked at the sandals on his feet. He then shuffled out of them and gazed at the attacker.

"I have only these, but if you wish, I would gladly give them."

The aggressor stepped back a step and shrugged embarrassingly. Confused feelings ran through him as he tried to pull together the thrust the incident had taken.

"Listen, man," he said, waving his hand in bewilderment. "Keep it. I don't want anything from you."

The mugger was totally disarmed by the Messenger's manner.

"But you do," the Messenger returned. "You wanted a thing more precious than gold. Rarer than the finest jewels."

The mugger's confusion began to turn to curiosity, "You mean you know where some of that stuff can be had?"

"My friend. All those things pass away. Where there are precious jewels, there will be no more. Where there is gold, it shall fall by the way. But I speak of a thing that shall never pass away."

"You talk like my grandmother used to talk," the mugger said skeptically but still fascinated.

"Your grandmother was a good woman, Mark."

The aggressor wielded back in total surprise.

"How did you know my name?"

"Because of my mission, I know many things. I know you loved your grandmother. I know she took care of you in your younger days. I know the pain and the loneliness you felt when she died. Struck down in the streets by a maimed man much as yourself."

The mugger stood transfixed as his mind floated on the words of the Messenger. They were days he'd forgotten. Days he'd long buried in the back of his mind. Whispers of a past that he would rather not remember.

"Hey, Dog!" a tall slender youth cried out from the end of the block.

He and two other toughs ran toward the Messenger.

"What's happening here?" the youth questioned as he stopped next to the mugger.

Mark silently studied his three companions. He suddenly felt odd. Like he didn't fit with the rest of the three.

"What's wrong with you, Dog? Why you lookin' so weird?" the tall slender youth asked.

"I thought you were going to make the hit and split," added another.

"This ain't the only trick on the streets," the slender one chimed in. "If he ain't got no cash, just snuff him out. We got a lot of grounds to cover."

"Yeah, Dog. What's wrong with you?" another added.

Mark did not know what to say. He wanted to stay and listen to the words of this strange man, yet his friends were beckoning him.

"Where's your blade, man?" one asked.

The others were shocked, for it was a cardinal code of the streets to never lose control of your weapon. They looked around and saw his knife on the crate next to the Messenger.

"He took your blade. Take this fool out!" the slender youth yelled as he pulled out a switchblade and made a move for the Messenger. Mark's heart leaped at the thought of his violent companion harming this stranger; a man, in only a few short moments he had somehow come to know.

"No!" he screamed and tackled the slender youth at the legs. The other two toughs fell to the ground and grabbed at Mark's limbs in an effort to subdue him.

While the four of them scuffled, they heard a dead flat clink. The noise was not loud but it had an annoying ring to it, almost like fingernails on a blackboard. They all looked around and saw Mark's blade wobbling end to end, stuck halfway into the concrete. The eyes of the four widened in astonishment at the sheer feat of it. The Messenger stood over them, appearing as tall and awesome as the tallest redwood. His voice bolted out with authority, the likes of which they had never known.

"This will not endure!" he thundered. "You do this! Murderers! You do this and live."

The four slowly untangled and got off the ground. They were mesmerized by the resonance of the Messenger's voice.

"But know you not," the Messenger continued, "that you will die?"

"You, Raymond," the Messenger said swiftly pointing at the muscular youth. "As your father fell victim, pushed from the roof of a building by one seeking the pleasures of the flesh. And you, Mark. Your grandmother shot by a criminal at the night. Know you all that you will likewise die?

"The savage hatred. The lust. Greed shall never be quenched. Those who have sought your mercy and have not seen it. The blood cries out!"

"No!" Mark screamed as he put his hands over his ears.

While the Messenger talked, a few onlookers gathered near to see what the commotion was about. Among them was the cripple who had been selling pencils across the street and the two prostitutes. They were shocked by what they saw; for the youths had terrorized the neighborhood for years. Break-ins, muggings, rapes, even murders were suspected at the hands of these young men. And here was this bearded stranger, speaking in an odd manner to the thugs, and they seemed affected by it.

"The knife you see before you," the Messenger demanded to point to the knife half stuck in the concrete, "can you take that knife? Can you plunge it into the belly of another? Watch blood spill, by your own hands, and be proud? No! You cannot. For the evil which persists out of you hates not those you kill, you hurt, you ruin. As much as it hates you!

"You destroy not because it gives you pleasure, but because it gives you rage. You maim not because you delight in violence, but because it causes you pain. You murder not because you lust for blood, but you lust for blood because you hate yourself!

"Now, die if you will, doers of evil!"

The Messenger reduced his voice to a low whining deliberate drawl, which cut through the hearts of everyone listening.

The slender youth was so unnerved that he screeched in a frightening panic, not wanting to hear any further. Gritting his teeth tightly, he closed his eyes and raced at the Messenger in a blind rage.

The Messenger relaxed in confidant authority and looked to his side at arm's length of the attacking youth. He raised his arm and thrust out his hand at the raging young man.

"Stop!" he commanded. "Come no further!"

The sound pierced the boy's ears, and he looked up and saw the hand of authority outstretched and unyielding. The young man could not raise his will over that of the Messenger. He felt his knees weaken, and the slender youth was compelled to stop. He then dropped to his knees in the middle of the sidewalk and began weeping like a baby. As a few more bystanders collected, the Messenger stood up on one of the wooden crates.

"We seek the comforts of this world," the Messenger called out to the small crowd which had gathered. "We seek fine clothes, mounds of riches. And yet, is the body not more than clothing? And the man more than riches? Precious few people knew the riches that are within their grasps. In haste to please the outer man, the inner man is lost. Lost in a bed of confusion and misery by the same hands that reach out for better things. Mankind, you are reaching for peace. Contentment. Satisfaction. Things that are good for you. Which are right for you. It is good. But you desire a crust of bread and read for a scorpion. You seek a refreshing drink of water and reach for a viper's poison. If we seek contentment, it cannot be found in a warehouse. It does not have a retail price.

"Contentment is not measured in success or failure. Contentment cannot be supplied in the pleasures of this world.

"No! They are opposites. If you seek peace, if you want contentment; loosen your grip on the selfish hoardings in your lives, so that you can be free to grab hold of your treasures when it comes."

The small crowd hung on to every word that the Messenger was saying. It was not so much the content, but the way in which he said the words. The firmness and compassion he seemed to emanate by his very presence. Each individual felt as if he were talking to them alone. But among the crowd which gathered, there were some skeptics. Those who had long since given up believing in anything.

"Yeah!" said Sid, the cripple, holding the cup of pencils. "Show me some money! If you fill this cup, I can buy anything I don't have."

The Messenger looked out into the crowd in the direction of the cripple, "Can you?"

"You keep the inner contentment. Just give me the outer cash!" the cripple joked sarcastically.

The crowd's transfixed state was broken for a moment by the raw humor and some began to laugh.

"Yeah!" one of the prostitutes called out. "I feel really peaceful when my pocketbook is full."

The crowd laughed loudly again. The Messenger stood silent, casting a burning gaze at the cripple. He slowly raised one arm and extended his hand toward the prostitute. The small crowd which were gaining stragglers and passers-by wounded at the Messenger's silence and slow movement. He appeared so graceful and at peace in everything he did.

"My hand is full," the Messenger said to the prostitute, not taking his eyes off the cripple…"of life," came the conclusion of his statement after pausing just long enough.

"Ha!" cried the cripple. "That and quarter couldn't get you a shot of Grandad!"

"Could it buy you your health?" the Messenger asked.

The cripple blinked, stunned for a second by the Messenger's question.

"You who labored your whole work-life faithfully for a tireless firm who cared little for you. They paid you well for your services. And yet, where did that pay lead you? Where are your riches now that you need them? When your limb was destroyed in the mechanism ill-fitted by that same tireless firm who did not care; and in the act of doing your job, your limb was crushed, could all the riches in the world give you back your leg?"

The cripple's mouth began to quiver at the memory of it. His face broke down in a saddened, defeated expression. He was both hurt and shocked at how this particular man could have known and at the same time that he might bring up so painful a memory.

"A great injustice was done you," the Messenger continued. "Had not that accident happened to you, you would have been in a different place. Yet to the glory of God, you are here! Come forward."

The cripple dropped his cup of pencils and limped to the Messenger.

"You speak of riches, and of wealth. If your life could change now; what would you really wish deep beyond all wishes?"

The cripple had tears in his eyes. He stammered incoherently, but his meaning was clear. That he might walk.

The Messenger stepped from the crate. As he did, the crowd moved in closer around him. They pressed against each other, some jumped up and down in the rear to catch a glimpse of what was happening.

"Take your crutch and cast it aside," the Messenger commanded.

He then motioned the cripple to lay down on the sidewalk. The cripple clearly didn't understand but willingly obeyed. The Messenger then looked up before the entire crowd. He held both hands' palms upward and spoke almost in a whisper.

"As a light in the darkness shines in the life of this life, let it be complete. In accordance with your will and in your way."

He then knelt down on one knee and touched the crippled man's leg.

"Be now whole."

As the words of the Messenger went forth, the cripple felt a tingling sensation in a leg he'd felt nothing in for years. He felt a pulling pressure, and he reached down to touch it and could feel the pressure of his fingertips over the surface. His eyes grew wide open and he sat up in startling realization.

"Stand, my friend, and walk," the Messenger proclaimed.

Low, hushed mumbles of excitement came from the crowd as the cripple leaned back on his hands and wobbly stood up. He stretched his leg out and put pressure on it. The leg totally supported him. His steps were a bit uneasy because he hadn't used two legs for so long, but he walked around and around excitedly in circles.

"Oh my! Oh my God!" the cripple exclaimed. "It's healed! I'm well!"

He jumped up in the air and fell on the sidewalk in the clumsy newness of it all.

A jolt of excitement shot through the crowd and isolated individuals began to step forward.

"I had a busted hand when I was younger. My thumb grew crooked," the muscular tough who had insulted him earlier spoke out.

The Messenger placed his hand over the crooked thumb. When he pulled it away, the thumb was straight.

The crowd began to press in on the Messenger with pains and illnesses; while he taught and healed as many as he would. People left and came back with friends and relatives to see this strange miracle worker. They listened intently to the words he said. Soon, a large crowd had gathered around the spot and the overflow was blocking some cars which were trying to get through the street.

Overhead, two officers spotted the scene in an LAPD security service chopper and radioed the event back to headquarters.

"This is KG37R security to base. We have a large crowd gathered in the vicinity of the Langdon Warehouse that could be a riot, but hostile action doesn't appear to be ongoing at this time. Over."

There was a fuzzy hush and a clicking sound on the remote.

"We got you 37R. Can you give us a description of the crowd? Is there any organized movement?"

"Ah…negative," came the answer from the chopper. "There seems to be one individual and an overflow. Almost resembles some type of rally."

"We'll send it out to dispatch, 37. They'll put some squads on it. We'll check it out."

"I'm going to swing in for a closer look. I'll notify any changes. KG37R security out."

Two LAPD squad cars were called and arrived at the scene of the crowd from different directions. As the officers got out, they saw the people in a fan-like a pattern broadening out from the point where the Messenger stood. One younger boy on the outer edges of the crowd which had flowed over from the street to the other sidewalk, snatched a woman's purse and darted down an alley. The officers couldn't afford to chase him. They had orders to get to the bottom of the crowd.

The policemen drew their guns and began to head toward the front. As they forced their way through, hostile reactions came from some of the bystanders. When they got to the front, they were surprised to see four young men sitting in front of a bearded man with a crowd intently listening to his instructions.

"Hey! That's Dog and his boys," one of the stunned officers said.

"Alright! Alright!" the elder officer, gun pointed, addressed the Messenger. "What's going on here?"

The Messenger stopped speaking, and the people close to him focused on the officers.

The Messenger stood up and addressed them.

"Your eyes do not deceive you. As you see. So also, it is. No more."

Some other wanderers who were attracted by the crowd began to tamper with the police cars, some began rocking the cars back and forth, and one husky man wrestled with one of the squad lights until it broke off the top of the car.

Moments later, a police van pulled up with a riot squad in police gear. Six officers with long batons, white gloves, white boots, and helmets filed out if the micro-bus. They quickly advanced on the group gathering around the police cars. The squad strode with complete confidence, straightway. Then, they came closer, many of the group instantly backed away. Some of the more stubborn ones were pushed away by the policemen holding the batons in front of them with two hands.

The riot squadron then turned its attention on the assembled crowd. There was much less resistance to the helmeted enforcers as they moved quickly to the front.

When they got through, they saw four youths and two blue-uniformed policemen sitting on the ground. The officers' guns were lying beside them as they listened intently to the bearded figure.

"Officer Hodges!" the captain of the riot police called out.

Both men in blue looked around, startled, and scrambled up off the ground. The people along the front laughed slightly at the rumpled behavior of the two beat cops.

"What is the meaning of this?" the captain demanded.

The captain then pushed the officers aside, his authority being very pronounced in full riot gear, and stared at the Messenger who was obviously the center of attention.

"Do you have a permit of assembly?" he asked, screaming aggressively at the Messenger.

"Only that this mass may listen," the Messenger replied.

"Well, that's not good enough," came the harsh response from the captain. "We're going to have to break this up."

He turned and faced the crowd.

"Alright, everybody! Let's break this up!"

The people at the front of the crowd stood firm, not wanting to leave. The helmeted riot squad turned and faced the crowd, readying themselves to apply force if necessary.

"Let's break this up!" the captain shouted once again.

A couple of voices at the rear of the crowd began to shout back at the riot police.

There were angry verbal exchanges, and then the people started to move in on the police. The Messenger stepped up on the crates once more and raised his hands.

"Please!" he responded. "We must be sensitive to each other."

The crowd slowly began to calm down again, and the captain turned around and marveled at the control the Messenger seemed to have over the people.

"As you wish," the Messenger stated. "I shall move on."

When he stepped down, a reporter rushed at the Messenger with a microphone connected to a tape recorder.

"Is it true, sir, that you healed an arthritic man this afternoon?"

The reporter's hat dropped from his head as he struggled to force the microphone in the Messenger's face. He was held back by the police, and the Messenger, not responding, walked on down the block.

The four youths followed him along with certain others of the crowd while the rest of the assembled mass began to disperse, a few at a time, edged on by the riot squad.

Some cameras clicked as the Messenger walked. Other reporters, who had picked up on the story from police dispatch, were already on the scene, attempting to get at the man who had a swirl of people around him.

The Kellys family had finished dinner and Linda was in the kitchen, washing dishes, while Charles looked over the evening's paper, sipping coffee. The television was on, but he only casually glanced up periodically.

On evening news broadcast from a live microwave remote, a newsman began to speak over a mini-cam, telling the story of the healings in the street and the unusual disturbance that caused. Live, they showed shots of the Messenger making his way in a swarm of people. They then interviewed several witnesses to the events.

Charles took a sip of coffee and finished a commentary on nuclear arms development.

He looked up at the TV screen and saw the Messenger making his way down a city block.

"Ann!" he shrieked excitedly, picking up the control and turning it up to high volume.

A dish broke in the kitchen as Ann rushed out to see what the matter. Charles pointed to the television screen.

"It's him? The Messenger!"

Ann gazed at the screen and put her hand over her mouth.

"Oh my God! It is!"

Just as Ann watched the tail end of the segment, it concluded.

The newsman at the anchor desk joked about swamis and gurus and then introduced the weather segment.

Picking up the remote-control, Charles turned the volume way down.

"I know he simply hadn't disappeared," Charles said, slightly smiling with reassurance.

"I went and searched for him in the hospital today, and there was nobody there," Ann added. "I had heard some rumors about his unusual physique, but it was nothing I could substantiate. He never checked out officially. He simply seemed to disappear."

"And now," Charles said slowly, "the healings and the crows. It's starting to turn into something. I can feel it."

Ann sat down on the couch next to Charles and put her arm around him, putting her head on his shoulder.

"It's incredible, Charles. I know that somehow this stranger…This Messenger is the pivotal point in a day that might perhaps change forever."

Charles consoled his wife by drawing her closer to him. What she said sounded so extreme and yet so absolutely true.

The next morning at the office, Charles anxiously gathered all of the news material he could find on the Messenger and any event surrounding him. He checked every morning's newspaper he could get his hands on, the teletype machine, the wire services, and the cable news outlet. There were spares segments and, clips here and there and for some reason, Charles could detect that story was already gaining momentum. He even found a piece of the world cable news network about it.

Charles, armed with his findings, walked down to the end of the newsroom and knocked on the city editor Melvin Le Clair's office. He heard a faint 'come in' and entered the rather cramped office with stacks of paper everywhere. Melvin Le Clair was a slightly built man with a black head of hair and busy pair of glasses, which slid down his nose often.

"I need some help, Melvin," Charles said.

Le Clair was sitting behind a metal desk and was shuffling slowly through a file of papers. He looked up at Charles over his glasses.

"What can I do for you, Kellys?" he asked.

"Look at these," Charles said, throwing the stories about the Messenger on Le Clair's desk one by one as if piling up some kind of case.

"What is this?" Le Clair asked, not knowing what to make of it.

"This story," Charles said. "It's heating up. It's a great piece for a city feature. Here's this man who comes out of nowhere attracting all this attention."

Le Clair picked up an article and studied a picture of the Messenger.

"So? Hippie guru comes to town. Big deal."

"Not a guru, Melvin," Charles intoned. "But a man of vision. A man who will guide the people from their misery."

"What kind of crackpot showmanship are you pulling, Kellys? Aren't you in enough hot water after balking over that military thing?"

"Please, Melvin," Charles pleaded. "I want this story."

"Why?" Le Clair asked. "What are you going to do with it?"

"Bring out the hidden facts. It's a city piece. This man is going to grow in importance Melvin. It's a hunch I have, and he's right here in our city. Think of what a shame it would be if the story is a rating winner and our station was last to get in on it?"

Le Clair glanced at some of the articles on his desk.

"What did you say his name was?" he asked.

"I don't know," Charles answered. "Nobody knows. That's what makes this scoop so attractive. A mysterious figure who all of a sudden becomes the center of a movement."

"This is crazy!" Le Clair said. "I shouldn't trust you after that stunt you pulled the other day, but I'll give you a chance."

"Thank you!" Charles stated in total gratitude. "It'll make a great feature."

"This is strictly a low budget operation, Kellys," Le Clair warned. "Only you and a tape disc. I give my authorization. But if you screw up, don't even bother to ask me for another favor."

"I won't. I won't," Charles said excitedly. "You won't be sorry."

"No Kellys I won't be sorry; but if you mess up…you will be."

"I won't," Charles stated again.

He began to pick up the articles from Le Clair's desk.

"Leave some of those. I want to read a little about his character."

Charles took the articles he had in his hands and left the office. Going back to his desk, he took out his tape machine and plugged in a fresh disc. He packed the extra things he thought he might need in his briefcase and headed for the elevator.

On his way to the car, Charles rethought his incredible first encounter with the visitor. He remembered his deep revealing eyes and his very pronounced yet graceful appearance. It was an experience he would never forget.

He got into his car and searched through the newspaper articles for places he might go find the Messenger. Deciding on a likely spot, Charles then started the car. He wheeled out of the studio a lot prepared for the assignment. Charles had to pass through areas of the inner city, a thought that he did not relish, but his desire to see the stranger again was stronger than a reluctance to travel through those unsavory areas. Locking his door upon entering the less stable neighborhood, he avoided as many lights as he could while experiencing only minor incidents. Two street gangs embattled with each other had poured their rage into the street, and Charles felt the head of a rival gang member being slammed repeatedly against the hood of his car. Another larger gang member pinned the youth to the hood. Charles sped off, knocking the two off the car. The scrimmaging warriors never seemed to notice him. On another occasion, he was flagged down and propositioned at the end of an alley for sex by the women, one of them wielding a baseball bat, but he was able to avoid incident by pretending he was letting them in and then quickly spinning off.

He finally reached the neighborhood that he was looking for. Charles cruised along until he spotted a crowd of people silently listening to a single distinct voice at the front. There were numerous newspaper and cameramen around, and a news helicopter from a cable station was circling propping a zoom lens out of his passenger compartment.

Charles got out and hoisted himself up on the roof of his car to get a better car shot of what was being said. The voice was unmistakable, and his ears felt somehow as hungry as the rest of the listeners for what was being said.

"This world has been weighed in the balance and found wanting," the Messenger said. "We add up the lives of the people who have yielded increase and those who have come to naught, and the scales tip. Then it is for us who live to assume the right and the judgment of those who have gone before us. If we are in any way at fault, we can blame only ourselves.

"In this world, wickedness abounds and it is encouraged to remain plentiful. Rewards for producing and devising evil plans are weaved into the fabric of the very societies themselves. Hatred and divisions are encouraged by social systems. Injustice cause the propagation of crimes and criminals. Cheating, backstabbing, treachery receive rewards in the economic systems and thusly down the line until there is no chance for the truth to prevail. Without avoiding the truth, a person cannot proceed to make their mark. Lies become our partner. We must deceive and be deceived in order to fulfill our day. How long? How long in our world must this persist? Will this continue unabated throughout eternity? Your wisdom tells you that it will not."

As the Messenger spoke, a long black limousine with a small entourage following pulled up. The newsmen's cameras began clicking in that direction. Security people dressed in black suits began to file out of the other cars gathered around the large black car. Many of the people on the edge of the crowd pointed and talked among themselves about the limousine.

A reporter looked at license plates that read simply J.S. When the door to the limousine was opened, John Spaulding emerged in dark shades, wearing a beige three-piece business suit.

"That's John Spaulding, the industrialist!" one reporter shouted.

Spaulding's security moved the on-lookers out of the way as he strided up to the front where the Messenger stood. He kissed the Messenger's hand and knelt down on one knee.

"John, my friend."

The Messenger stepped down the crate and lifted Spaulding from the ground.

Squad cars with lights flashing started to emerge around the swelling crowd.

The reporters began calling back to their respective stations with stories and pictures of John Spaulding and the Messenger. Some of the stragglers who were not with the main body threw bottles and rocks at the police.

Charles watched the Messenger and the industrialist speak amidst the swirling crowds and media people. At the other end of the block, the police battled troublemakers, chasing them down and throwing them into tank-like paddy wagons at a far comer.

In the meantime, the stories the reporters were sending out only emphasized the impact this stranger was having. Charles overheard a radio report in which people told of life-changing experiences. While, still other reports of healings and even taped manuscripts of his words were being sent forth. The biggest story, however, was of the influential industrialist paying homage to the Messenger.

John Spaulding tried to press an envelope packed with money on the strange visitor, but he refused it.

"I do not want money," the Messenger stated gratefully, "only that you remember and never forget, as you have experienced in your heart. Never deny that."

A reporter made his way past the perimeter of the people close to the two in front.

"Mr. Spaulding," he said quickly, trying to get in a question. "What is your connection with this man?"

His security people knocked the microphone back and tried to push the reporter aside.

"No!" Spaulding commanded. "Let him through."

The reporter stepped forward, repeating his question.

"I have no shame," Spaulding pronounced. "Truly, this is a great man of God. When I lay in the hospital dying of cancer, this man healed me in the night. It is for that that I am eternally grateful."

The reporter's eyes bulged because of the scoop he'd received. Many other media people within earshot dashed for phones to inform their communication bases of the latest. The people in the audience were equally surprised at the far teachings of the Messenger's works. Some cheered, while others, whose lives had been touched and changed by the Messenger, began to praise God.

At City Hall, the mayor was pulled out of a budgetary meeting by the vice-commissioner of the LAPD. The mayor was quite angry but compiled because of the emergency need for the council.

"It could already have hit," the voice commissioner stated.

"Hit? What are you talking about?" the mayor asked, not willing to beat around the bush.

"Code R. The city-wide panic. We're having trouble in the fourth district with a man nobody's ever seen or heard of before," he continued.

"You come to me with a simple problem like that? Just arrest him or have him taken out by some other means you, fool!" the mayor said angrily.

"Your honor, I'm afraid it's not that simple. This man is reportedly healing people. I can't directly confirm how, but the public is eating it up. Condition Code R has not occurred yet, but if we do anything to him; that might set it off."

The mayor put his hand over his mouth, thinking for a moment.

"How long have we had teams trained and ready for the Code R crisis?"

"It's been seven years now since we received the report from the Rank Think Tank on city-wide panic. We built our contingency pilot in six months, so I'd say a good five years."

"Who's in charge of the project right now?" the mayor fired another question.

"Mayor Robert Tynan, a specialist in urban tactics sir," the vice-commissioner promptly answered.

"I'm going to finish this meeting. You get Tynan, Williams, and the commissioner to my office in an hour. In the meantime, I want this man covered like a hawk. Keep him shadowed constantly."

The mayor turned and paused.

"Ah…also; keep the word down and try to divert people away from him."

"We can't, sir," the vice-commissioner said. "The character has a penchant for public speaking. He's got crowds around him all the time now."

"Well, bust it up," the mayor demanded.

"We've been trying sir, but the people become enraged whenever we do. The last time we did this morning; there was some isolated burning and looting but we were able to contain it,"

"Alright! Alright!" the mayor gave in. "Let it alone for now. But keep him covered and get those people to my office in an hour."

The mayor then returned to the meeting.

The Messenger walked down several blocks with the press and hundreds of people following him. Many curious observers stared from building windows trying to get a glimpse of him. Numerous disabled were veterans, sufferers of incurable diseases, and permanently injured citizens who had heard and lined the streets in hopes of gaining a cure.

The Messenger stopped in front of a large gray stone church. Saint Anthony's Parish stuck out most obviously among the tenements of the poor around it.

Looking out of a window in the church's balcony was a priest who immediately ran toward the rectory to alert the pastor.

The Messenger walked up the steps and stood before the huge wooden doors. He turned, facing the crowd after tugging on the locked entrance.

"Behold, a house of worship! This is my testament," the Messenger proclaimed. "That is the solace of the sanctuary, the time schedule of man has been imposed.

"I show this to the people and declare it unto you that you might know the hour is at hand. Even at the door. Perhaps yourselves lost flock."

The pastor put a call through to his superiors downtown very quickly, seeking instructions from the central office. He was surprised to get the rector of Los Angles the cardinal himself on the phone.

"I'm curious about this man and his manner," the cardinal stated.

"Your excellency, I have only an impoverished, district parish. I don't want any trouble," the pastor nervously replied.

"I understand your position, Father," the cardinal said, rather coolly. "Tell you what, this afternoon, in about an hour, there is to be a luncheon with some World Council representatives attending. I and a bishop from the Episcopal faith were talking about this man over dinner just last night. He is obviously a leader of distinguishing qualities. I would like for him to attend our luncheon. I'll arrange for a limousine to pick him up there at your parish. What I want you to do is to inform him of my request and seek approval. I'll make the rest of the arrangements. Is this clear Father?"

"Yes, your excellency," the priest obeyed.

The Messenger informed the crowd about the rudiments of a house of worship. While talking, the pastor, who was a slightly overweight balding man, came from around the side of the church with two priests at his side and advanced toward the Messenger.

By the time he'd made his way through the crowd, the reporters and the other media people; the pastor was very frightened. He was afraid to look up at the Messenger who was looking softly out at this approach.

"UH…" the pastor began, not knowing his name. "Teacher, my superiors request your person at a luncheon. It is hoped that you might honor our invitation with your presence."

The Messenger lifted the pastor's chin with his hand and peered into his eyes. The two priests beside him took a couple of cowering steps back. The Messenger saw the fear within the pastor.

"Who is superior to you, my friend?" he asked kindly. "Who are all but parts of a body. The hand is no greater than the foot. I will go to the meal as you have asked."

The pastor was taken off guard by the mild manner of the Messenger.

"I will inform my superior of your acceptance," the pastor said. "You are invited into our rectory to await your private car."

"There is no need. Here, I am needed," the Messenger thankfully responded.

The priests then returned to the rectory building as the Messenger sat on the steps, talking to a group of the aged he had called before the crowd. A white limousine slowed to a stop in front of the church, dispersing the overflow. A priest dressed in all black got out and went through the crowd up to the Messenger.

"Uh, sir," he addressed politely. "I have your car."

Getting up without saying another word, the Messenger went out into the street and climbed into the limousine. There was a hushed sound of muffled voices from the crowd as the limousine driver accelerated away.

The dining room was a posh elegant spot with several waiters and the most expensive silver and china in a beautiful setting. All of the most important high church officials in the city met each week to communicate and sandal ideas, socialize, and to cement a stronger bond between the faiths. The various members of all men of advanced years stood randomly around the table, lightly chattering in the wait of their guests.

Finally, a bell was sounded, and the door was opened. A rather unsophisticated figure walked in, in a very drab sackcloth outfit with unshaven face and sandals. He was a striking contrast to the opulence around him. The Messenger stared in wonder at all of the beautifully arrayed trappings around him.

The table bell was rung, and the guests took their places. The Messenger was showed a seat at the end of the table next to the cardinal. An opening prayer was offered by a Methodist bishop.

"Lord, we thank you for the food we are about to receive. Thank you for this occasion. Help us, this body to build unity and understanding not only among ourselves but throughout the world. We pray Amen."

There was a follow of an "Amen" by the rest of the group with the exception of the Messenger. They then sat down and shook their linen napkins open, setting them in their laps. The Messenger studied their motions and did as they did.

The cardinal leaned over as the Methodist bishop read the minutes.

"I'm glad you could come. I'm going to introduce you to the body. What is your name?"

The Messenger glanced at him calmly, "I am a Messenger come. That I might bear a certain passage."

"And now we have Cardinal Thomas Nhielman to introduce guest…"

There was a shorthand clap as the cardinal stood up.

"Members of this distinguished body. A very unusual man has come to the attention of myself and indeed this entire city almost overnight. Some of the works he has been said to have done are nothing short of miracles. This interesting man in such a very short time is attracting tremendous amounts of attention. Because his work is also of a religious nature, I thought it appropriate to bring him before us. I am grateful that the opportunity to have him arose, and I am grateful his attendance could be arranged. Therefore, colleagues and members of the World Council, I give you," he then paused hesitantly and looked aside, "a Messenger."

The group began to look at each other in question. They whispered the name and shrugged shoulders as to what it meant. The cardinal sat down and leaned over once again.

"You are to speak," he said to the visitor.

The Messenger stood up slowly, and his rising commanded attention by its very act.

"I am a Messenger."

"A Messenger of what?" came a question from a Lutheran bishop.

"A Messenger of the truth," came the visitor's answer.

"Who sent you? What faith do you profess?" another official asked.

"I'd profess nothing," the Messenger answered. "I am and have come for a walk this day sent by one who is greater than I."

"A walk?" a Baptist minister questioned. "A Messenger? You're not making any sense. What church do you come from? Catholic, Protestant, Evangelical, some cult, give us some answers?"

The Messenger looked at the man arching his eyebrows but saying nothing.

"Well, what philosophy do you expose?" came an enquiry from a Fundamentalist preacher. "What is your position on the virgin birth? Do you teach water baptism?"

The Messenger took in all the questions and stepped back.

"You question me on things of small matter. You who are responsible for the lives of millions can entertain yourselves in such splendor, while those who look to you do without. You, who toss questions on issues which feather the ear and tickle the mind delight in quizzical abstraction, making a language unto yourselves while the needy do without and the lost wander ever farther. Vipers! Your many riches and good living are not attained by your own hand. Do not think that this state goes unnoticed. For I tell you, for every laborer, there is a wage!"

Catholic Monsignor was outraged by the lack of respect shown by the Messenger. "Young man!" he bolted up, demanding, "What right do you have addressing our highly respected body in this manner? Show us your authority to make such accusation!"

The Messenger threw his linen napkin down and stormed toward the door. He pivoted at the room's threshold.

"I'll show you nothing but the sign of the days before the flood. For as in those days, men ate and drank and were merry knowing not until the flood came and took them all away!" With that, he turned for his final exit.

The Catholic Monsignor threw his napkin down and walked over to the other side of the room, fuming. The other members were buzzing noisily about the exchange.

"I told you it might be trouble," an Episcopalian told the cardinal. At the same time, the limousine driver approached the cardinal, motioning for information. The cardinal signaled him to attend to the Messenger. Running out into the lobby, the driver caught him entering the street.

"I have been instructed to assist you in your way," he said. "Where do you want to go?"

The Messenger turned and looked at him, "From where I have come."

Chapter 12
The Third Day

The day was just breaking over the shores of the Pacific Ocean. The sun beamed a bright yellow against the fluffy formation of clouds, hazed by the prevailing morning smog which clung to the balmy Los Angeles atmosphere. The faint chatter of a flock of honking geese could be heard flying low above the city.

The Messenger walked down a skid row street swarmed by a couple of hundred followers. Some had their whole lives changed by his words. Others had experienced healings by his hands. Still, others were struck with spellbound curiosity by his acts and his manner. Several security officers kept their distance, keeping an eye on the incidents of the hour. They periodically checked in with the authorities. Most reporters stayed close, not wanting to miss any new development in the stir this man was causing.

The interest and curiosity in this strange visitor had grown to worldwide proportions. In only a short period of time, news bureaus from every corner of the globe had correspondents on the scene, interviewing people around him, collecting stories, and sending back footage of the great speaker and healer in their midst. People's hearts had grown so empty that this Messenger, who spoke with compassion saying things that people needed to hear, had become a wonder to all those upon whose ears his words fell. Transcripts of his speaking were sent out through news wire translated into various languages and run in the dailies of the people of every nation. It seemed that the entire world, at least at this moment, had become curiously transfixed by this strange bearded man.

On this particular avenue, there were several taverns, missions, and storefront churches. The religions practiced in these places ranged from marathon preaching to snake handling. The Messenger walked in silence, not answering any of the calls to him by the needy who lined the streets to get a blessing from him. There were aged and crippled people lying on the tops of cars, reaching out and calling to him. As he gazed at the masses, he pained deeply. He wanted to touch many more, but his mission was clear, and he could not alter his path.

When he came to the end of the block, he turned the corner and faced a red brick congregational church. It was rather large with three round stained-glass windows along the sides of the building. The lawn area was unkept and some of the railings leading to the door were broken from the mooring. A few feet above the doorjambs, in blaring red letters, a banner was strung.

BIG GALA LAS VEGAS WEEKEND!
24 HOUR BINGO   PARAMUTUAL TABLES

PLAY OUR VIDEO RACES
24 HOUR DAILY   2 EVERY HOUR

The Messenger looked at the sign and then firmly walked up the stairs. Some of the followers went up behind him while others who were still filing around the corner filed up the street in front of the building.

As the Messenger entered, he saw an attendant dozing in a tall chair by a registering stand in the rear of the vestibule. Two women stood by the main room door, nonchalantly talking and exchanged bingo cards. Upon noticing a commotion, the women were startled by the seriousness of the bearded man being followed in reverence. There were decorations around the lobby with posters of casinos hung along the walls to give an air of Las Vegas to the happening.

Opening the door to the church itself, the Messenger looked at pews which had been pushed aside to make room for long tables. The tables occupied most of the center of the room space. There were a dozen or so players at the different tables, some lay face down, sleeping after a long night, while others, intent on making that last score, played on. As he watched the action, a very large well-dressed man, standing by the door, turned neatly, addressing him.

"Paramutual tables are to your left. You can pick up your cards two for five dollars at the table in the far corner. Our video races are fun every half-hour. If you want to split on the daily double…"

While he was talking, a neatly dressed minister strided down the aisle and clasped his hands together with a wide smile.

"Don't you know who this is, Cleatus? This is our friend who had been so much on the news lately," the minister called out. "Come in. Come in. Bring all your friends with you. We'll give a free complimentary card to everyone. Be our guest."

The Messenger walked past the minister and over to the table where contestants were still playing. He watched as the cage on the green tablecloth was spinning, and a number came up.

"T-39," the spinner called out.

"Bingo!" screamed one woman excitedly, holding up her hand pointing to the card.

The minister saw the disgruntled expression on the Messenger's face and felt compelled to give an explanation.

"It's a charity drive," he offered. "To help raise money for the pastor's trip to the Holy Land."

Incensed, the Messenger looked at the minister, "You speak of charity while you foster greed. Raising up the hopes and capitalizing on the dreams of the poor, that they might win, you offer only despair. If this sanctuary were used for prayer and steadfastness, my father is praised. But you do not consecrate this house as it is meant to be, you make it a den of thieves!"

The Messenger then boldly and angrily turned over a bingo table.

"Thieves! Vipers! Remove yourselves from this house!"

Players around the tables jumped up in fear and looked hesitantly at the chips and money rolling on the floor. The Messenger then began turning over all the gambling tables in the room.

"Come out! Cast your wickedness aside your laborers of doom! I will not have this sanctuary made a mockery by your evil deeds. Leave this abode."

There was pandemonium and confusion as people scattered in every direction. Some dove for money, others headed for the door. There was screaming, and panic at the behavior of this seemingly mad man.

Cleatus, the large man by the door, came at the Messenger but found a table thrown between them.

"This is a house of worship. Not a parlor for sinners!" he said, looking right into the face of the huge bouncer.

Cleatus stopped in his tracks. He hesitated for a moment. Even though the tables were being thrown by this man, he did not seem foreboding. There was a certain air of calmness that emanated from the Messenger, even in this tense state. This odd combination had an unnerving, almost frightening, quality about it as Cleatus stood, totally arrested by the Messenger's manner.

"Leave this place at once!" the Messenger shouted again, this time gently but firmly grabbing hold of the bouncer's elbow.

Cleatus rambled toward the door with a puzzled look on his face as the Messenger continued to turn the church out. He couldn't make a decision as to what to do and in the confusion of hastening people, Cleatus found himself doing no more than the rest of them.

Finally, the gambling area was a shamble. The Messenger knelt silently near the entrance of the sanctuary.

"My Lord and Master. Forgive them. The importance of your sanctuary is lost upon them. They are but sheep and have lost sight of the shepherd. Have mercy, Lord."

The Kellys family sat silently around the breakfast table. An early edition, with the headline reading MESSENGER SEEKS UNITY lay next to Charles's plate. In the morning's devotional, there had been such an electric charge generated by the events of the past two days that the family was emotionally drained afterward.

Ann watched the swirling motion made by the stirring of her office. Linda toyed with her cereal spoon. Charles thought about the whirlwind shape things concerning the Messenger were taking.

Ann took a sip of her coffee and pulled a folded note out of her bathrobe pocket.

"What's that?" Charles inquired.

"It's a note from the institute," Ann answered. "A summons from the district psychologist. We have to meet with him next Wednesday."

"What's this all about?" Charles asked, reaching for the note.

Ann handed it to him, "Something about a family disorder. They want to council us about Linda."

Charles folded up the note and tossed it to the middle of the table. He picked up the newspaper again and studied a revealing picture of the Messenger.

"They're writing us trivial letters like that when the biggest story the world has ever seen is taking place in our streets."

"Are you picking up on any new angles on your assignment?" Ann asked.

"I can hardly keep my mind on the fact that it is an assignment. Knowing what I know; the things he says and does are so fascinating," Charles responded.

"Have you told anybody else?" she questioned.

"I doubt if there would be anybody who'd believe me," Charles said, "and yet the things that he is doing."

Charles then looked down. He had to reveal an urge he could no longer keep in.

"Ann," he said quickly. "I know this sounds crazy. But let's not send Linda to school this morning. Why don't you stay home from work and the three of us go down to see him this morning?"

"What?" Ann was taken off guard. "Well, I don't know what to say."

"Let's do it, Ann. I've had this feeling all morning. I want Linda to see him and feel the sincerity and power with which he speaks."

Ann glanced at Linda, who was sitting on the edge of her chair. Her wide eyes pleaded with expectation.

"Uh…"

She started, torn between her responsibilities at the hospital and the desires of her family.

"Okay."

Linda jumped with excitement while Charles beamed a smile of satisfaction.

"Alright, I'll go," Ann stated again, this time sure of her answer. "But we'll have to call the school to excuse Linda. They already think something is wrong with us."

Charles rose up from his seat and folded the paper under his arm.

"It's settled then," he said, after taking one last sip of coffee. "I'll call the school while you and Linda finish up here."

Charles strolled over to the table phone in the living room and called to inform the attendance secretary of Linda's impending absence. He then went upstairs to get dressed for the family excursion. A trip to get a glimpse of what he surely thought was the most spectacular event to ever hit the city of Los Angeles. He laid his blue shirt out on the bed and went into the bathroom to throw some sprinkles on his oxford brown shoes.

Ann called the hospital and asked her superiors to find a substitute for the shift. She had to promise some extensive favors to convince her, but the request was granted. With that out of the way, she was soon dressed in a dark green skirt and plaid top with her mint green sweater over her arm.

The couple went down the hall met by Linda who was ready to go. Coming down the stairs and out the door, there was a mild air of excitement amongst the family. Linda had never seen the Messenger in person, but she knew about Charles's experience; while Ann had wanted to see again, ever since that first day at the hospital. Charles turned to lock the front door and, on a table, next to the entrance, was his briefcase with his tape machine, note pads, and photos. He reached for the case but then hesitated for a moment. He had a sudden odd feeling that he wouldn't need it. He then closed and locked the door behind him.

Getting into the car, Ann looked at Charles and saw he was carrying nothing. "You forgot your briefcase," she commented.

"I don't think I'll need it," Charles said.

There was silence for a second as Ann received Charles's premonition. He started the car and wheeled out of the driveway. Linda sat on the edge of the back seat, peering over her mother's shoulder in anticipation.

"We're going to have to go through the inner-city areas," Charles cautioned. "So, I want you to keep the windows up and sit close to the middle of the car. You remember the last time we went through there?"

Glancing over, he raised his index finger. "Linda," he instructed, "Remember, if something happens, don't grab hold of your mother the way you did before. If I have to accelerate in a hurry that could be very dangerous. If you feel yourself in any danger at any time, lay down on the floor."

After his instructions, Charles ramped onto the freeway and pushed on toward the middle of the city. Straight ahead of him, a cloud-shaped in the image of the cross was firmly fixed in the morning sky. He motioned toward Ann and found her intently staring at the same thing.

Charles turned off at the proper exit and braced himself, warning the family one last time of the necessary caution to be taken. He turned one corner and headed down a side street, trying to retrace the trip he'd taken earlier. As he drove there, was an eerie silence in the streets, and it didn't take them long to realize that the streets were almost deserted.

"What's going on?" Ann asked in amazement.

Linda sat looking out of her windows and all around her but seeing very few people.

"I don't know," came Charles's concerned answer. "Usually, these streets are filled with people."

"But there's hardly anybody out here," Ann added.

"I don't understand," Charles said.

As they drove down the nearly deserted streets, the family began to detect a low murmur at the very edge of their hearing. The sound was like that of muffled voices. But it was very low and seemed to be coming from every direction. Charles turned his car and headed down Wilshire Boulevard. As he did, he saw a helicopter pass very low overhead. Soon, he came upon a line of cars that continued up the way as far as he could see. There were numerous people lining the block moving back and forth, but the traffic was stopped cold.

"I don't know what's going on, but we're not going to get anywhere sitting here," Charles commented.

He double-parked his car to the side as best he could and got out, grabbing Linda's hand; Ann pressed close to this other side. The people seemed to be pushing for the center of activity at Mac Arthur Park a few blocks down. Charles saw pickpockets and purse-snatchers working for the crowd, and he drew his family close to him as they made their way.

"I don't know what's going on," Ann said, "but I'm not sure this was a good idea."

"Hold on, Ann," Charles tried to reassure. "We'll get where we're going in a few minutes."

Another helicopter flew overhead, this time coming low enough to send gusts of air down on the crow, raising up the dust and blowing some hats off as it went by. There were people jammed all around the Kellys family as Charles finally made his way to the corner of the third block. Their movement was getting more difficult and there were so many people around Charles that he could see nothing but the backs of people's heads. Spotting an over-turned car on its side by a light-post, Charles instructed Ann and Linda to wait by a building as the people forced their way passed her.

Charles struggled his way over to the car and then, using the rear axle, he pulled himself up the side of it. He looked out past the corner across the street to a park and his eyes widened at the most spectacular sea of humanity he had ever beheld. There were thousands upon thousands of people covering every square inch of the area coming in all directions as far as the eye could see. He looked in the distance on the other end of the park and saw a lone simple figure standing in the bandshell. Overhead, helicopters, and higher above, single and twin engine planes circled the area, flying in and out as if on shifts relaying messages. Charles called over to Ann and waved her to come. She struggled her way over to the wrecked car and Charles pulled Linda atop, sitting her squarely against the light post, and then helped Ann to the top.

When Ann reached it, she looked out at what seemed like literally millions of people and was aghast at the ground they covered. Charles knelt beside her, pointing out the Messenger in the bandshell. Linda was standing behind them after getting up to watch a low flying security helicopter simply hover above them. The guests of air blew their hair out of place and the whole atmosphere resembled some sort of frightening circus. It was as if all social order had been abandoned and everybody was waiting for the next step. The Messenger gazed at the mass of people before him. There were microphones from most news bureaus, domestic and foreign, in front of him. It was odd that in the sea of faces which had come out to hear him; he felt more alone than he had ever felt.

"I didn't plan this," he uttered to himself, the microphones picking up the sound of his voice. There was screeching, and technicians ran forward to adjust the equipment.

The Messenger went to the other side of the platform away from the mikes and raised his arms. Tears began to fall from his eyes. He could no longer hold the pain he felt for humanity.

"Mankind! Be lost no more!" he stammered.

A curious effect had taken place around the world in all the lands on every continent; the sky brightened that moment regardless of the time of day. The symbol of the cross that arched its path across the skies became more pronounced so that everyone who noticed could see it clearly.

The Messenger went back over to the microphones and braced himself behind them.

"My heart cries out for you, and my soul weeps," he said. "There is no longer a place in which to hide. Every act which is done in the most secret places is made known. So, I beg of you. Bear your soul to the one who is true. To the one who is faithful. Lend yourselves over to the goodness which is just beyond you. The misery you suffer can be gone. The darkness you stumble in can be lightened. Each of you as sheep lost unto itself, seek your way back. When you hear the words of truth, harden not your hearts. Do not protect your ears with your own vanity. It can no longer do you any good. Seek your help away from yourself. If you are the center of yourself, cast that down. Build not walls but doors."

His body shook, and the Messenger stumbled backward as if faint. There was a hushed noise from the thronging masses at the sudden involuntary motion. The Messenger then moved swiftly across the platform to the point where he'd stood before. As he raised his arms slowly, piercing darkness began to flood the skies. The crowd became nervous due to the apparent supernatural change taking place. Everyone could feel the atmospheric transition. It was as if time itself had stopped.

The same effect occurred across the face of the planet. The peoples from the small villages and industrial towns throughout Europe and Asia came outside and began to focus on the darkening skies and the cross which began to glow in the darkness. The citizens of Africa and the Far East were equally astonished by the peculiar effect. In South America and across the whole of the face of North America and the Arctic regions, men watched the change aghast. The darkness was a chilling penetrating one that seemed to right through the skin and engulf the very spine of all those who experienced it.

"Behold, I show you a miracle!" the Messenger said, his voice carrying loudly without the aid of microphones.

At that instant, a swirling funnel out of the sky formed around him. He stood there as a might form pronounced in every way as the funnel-like invisible tornado swirled about him. A glimpse of a shining reflection could be seen through the funnel. The glistening was like light dancing across the surface of the cellphone.

"Hear me!" the Messenger's voice rang out from his stance within the caught-up whirl. His voice inflection was different from any other he had used.

The words resounded with authority. And at that time, in every spot on every continent in the world, the words were heard. Regardless of what language the population spoke, each person heard the voice in the sky as if it was their language. At that moment, every ear was turned, and every eye was upward.

"The former things are past; and now I offer you a new way. Let every man that has an ear, let him hear. And let each heart who would listen be silent, for the hour has come."

Following the word 'come' there was a seismic atmospheric thump accompanied by a trailing off hiss. The word continued to echo in the minds of the frightened mass. The body of the Messenger was illuminated through the swirling funnel in the hazing darkness around him. He looked upward and closed his eyes.

"I am a witness," he thundered. "Life is as it never was. My passage I have bared. And at last, I give you a message. An overpast is upon you even at the door. Show your faith. Be obedient to this, my master's request. But if you choose not to obey, the life that is in you be in your own hands, for my testimony is true. Heed the warning.

"Gather food. Clothing. Ample water to drink and take SHELTER. Your shelter can be any structure of your choosing. Let it be known that wherever you choose, your obedience is what is important. On the four corners of your shelter, place the cross as your sign of faith. You can use any matter to make the sign. In this manner, when the overpast has ended, go now, for the time is near."

At the completion of the last sentence, the Messenger started to rise slowly off the platform in the swirling funnel, and as he rose, his image faded. The sky brightened as the echo of his last words continued to be heard after he had disappeared.

The audience watched his ascension and heard the fading sound dumbfounded. Translated frantically into most languages and dialects, the reinforced transmitted message only took minutes to sink into the ears of the world body. Then panic. People began to rush in every direction out of fear of the warning.

Around the bandshell in the park, the masses of spectators scurried, causing tangled bottlenecks at the street corners. Some people were trampled by the pushing, shoving madness to escape. Security helicopters that had been on the scene flew low, urging calm through loudspeakers, but it did little good.

Men, women, and children all around the world reached for anything available to tie into a cross form. The pandemonium flooded the streets as shops were broken into by massive crowds overpowering guards. The looters' bounty was food, clothing, and other goods to be used in the shelters.

Charles helped Ann off the car and then reached for Linda, who readily jumped into his arm. Charles held Linda's hand with Ann close to his side and gingerly sidestepped the running mobs en route to his car. Two blocks into their journey, the Kellys were barely missed by a plowing large car obviously owned by a wealthy man who hit two or three other people in his haste to depart. His car collided with a passenger filled pick-up truck at the next corner. Both vehicles were stopped cold with other pedestrians fighting to take control of the steering wheels.

Eventually, the Kellys made it to their Volkswagen which had been ransacked and pushed off to the side. Charles helped Ann open her bent door, and after a few difficult turns of the key has got his old faithful started. He carefully drove through and around the bedlam of the city streets, sometimes having to drive on the sidewalks to avoid the mishap.

One maddened motorist tried to force Charles from the freeway. He sped alongside and cut in front of him in an old rusted car in an attempt to force the Volkswagen into an overturned semi-trailer truck straddling the median ditch. Charles avoided the trouble by abruptly breaking and swinging on the other side of the burning vehicle in the middle of the oil slick roadway. The mad driver, having had his ambush foiled, trailed in the distance as Charles made his way back home.

Screams and ambulance sirens could be heard all over the city. The air-raid sirens had been turned on throughout the metropolis and calm was urged through radio broadcasts everywhere. The wild dogs and cats which roamed the city's alleys howled and ventured boldly out into the streets. All holds broke loose. The world went haywire.

In the Hollywood district, a derelict with a large bottle of wine sat on the ground next to a dumpster oblivious to it all. He twiddled away at some twigs around him in an intoxicated fumble. With some loose string, he fashioned crosses. He staggered up and slid two of his four newly made symbols under the dumpster at the corners while placing the other two wedged tightly in the corners at the top.

Charles put the battered car into the garage, and the exhausted family quickly went into the house.

Running into the kitchen, Charles pulled several butter knives from the drawer. He angled them into the shape of crosses and searched for tape but didn't find any. Suddenly, he remembered a roll of masking tape he'd picked up on his way home from work. It was in his briefcase. He went over to the table by the front door and grabbed it. He opened it hastily, searching for the masking tape, when all at once, he paused, looking at the items he was shuffling through. They were the popsicle sticks tied in a cross shape. More determined than ever, Charles took the crosses and went out to his garage. He picked up a hammer and four small nails and proceeded to nail the crosses to the corners of his house.

During this time, Ann pulled several blankets from the hall linen closet and brought them downstairs to the living room. Linda brought the pillows from their beds which her mother arranged neatly on the floor next to the couch. The Kellys family, with full conviction, prepared in every detail to heed the Messenger's warning call. Charles closed the shutters to the windows along with securing every possible entrance.

As the family went about this task, they heard noises of confusion from out in the streets. Car breaks screeched, gunshots could be heard along with the sirens of police cars and ambulances.

Charles sat on the couch to catch his breath. He glanced over at Ann who was holding Linda close to her. Ann did not look afraid, but she had a very concerned expression. Linda clung to her mother in fear. Getting up again quickly, Charles hugged a firm reassuring embrace around the two of them. He then double-checked the secured areas and put chairs against the front and back doors as an extra measure.

Returning to his family huddled there on the living room floor, Charles sat on the couch and turned on the television. He switched the remote over to the cable stations and tried to get the BBC which ran live newsreels from all over the world. The family sat spellbound as the cable flashes narrated by a British newscaster showed chaos in India, Singapore, Brazil, Australia, Japan, and even some footage from mainland China.

Charles dropped to his knees and folded his hands in front of him tightly as he prayed with deep intentions. Linda and Ann joined him. Over the TV set, local reports told of people being killed by roving bands of thugs; others were taken away by the absence of social restraint. Groups of ravagers combed neighborhoods, some joined by very respectable men and women on raping sprees. Still, others hung silverware, pencils, broken chair legs, and even bicycle handlebars on their homes, cars, vans, churches, or other sought out sanctuaries in observance of the Messenger's decree.

Women of the night and hustlers were on the streets trying to make a fast buck amidst all the confusion while others who simply did not believe went along as normal, thinking it would all blow over. There was a male peddler in the middle of a boulevard selling crosses for five dollars. Winoes and drug addicts broke into liquor stores and pharmacies stealing whatever they could carry.

Charles pressed the switch on the remote control and turned the TV off. Linda watched him with pain in her eyes while Ann changed positions on the floor. She leaned back and looked at Charles who was rubbing his fingers through his hair in a weary manner.

"What will we do Charles?" she asked.

"We will do what the Messenger said," Charles answered with resolve. He then slid over to his family, parting them, putting one arm around Ann and the other around his daughter.

Chapter 13
Wages of Reckoning

Two and a half days past and many persons of the shelters became impatient. Many who had been caught up in the unusualness and the excitement of it all began to revert to the skeptical state of mind they had always held as the memory of the Messenger began to fade with the days already. Some began to leave the sanctuaries, and a few, together with total nonbelievers, even drove through neighborhoods and declared over loudspeakers that the overpast was a hoax. This breakdown of faith prompted even more of the lukewarm followers to give up.

Around the world, the situation was the same. People began to drift out of their shelters to visit friends or to do wrong. Others went out and tried to rebuild their lives as they had been before as best they could. Waiting for some sign that the whole thing would just blow over.

A main branch bank vice president in a large downtown Los Angeles sat in an empty office dressed for work, flying paper airplanes across the room. He got an idea in passing and got the keys to the vault, opening it to stacks of currency. The vice president then went to the tellers' window and pulled out a couple of bags left at the desk. After filling the bags with as much paper money as he could stuff into them, he entered out into the street and headed for his car. As he walked, the impact of what he was doing began to dawn upon him. He looked down at all the money; the ease in which he could take it, and thought about all the money he had left. It was just all free. Suddenly, he was flushed with the fact that he was now rich and at the same time the worth and the worthlessness of it all. He reached one hand down in a bag and began to throw some money into the air.

"I'm rich!" he shouted. "I'm rich!"

Eyes watched from the shelters in the business district and the sight of all the money was too much for some of them to take. Some broke free from the shelters while some of the sparse wanderers in the street blocks down were attracted by the commotion that began around the businessman.

"Give me some of that money!" one man shouted, crossing the street and rushing at the banker.

Several people followed and soon the vice president found himself swamped with people clutching at him.

"It's mine! Stay back!" the banker shouted as he tried to fight off all of the hands clutching at him.

His bags were knocked from his hands up into the air, and the money floated down into the street. The money-hungry crowd scurried for the bills and fought each other like vicious dogs for the paper on the ground. The banker dived in but was kicked and punched in the mad scramble. Other passersby who couldn't get into the scramble thought better of it and entered into the bank. When the others saw this, they jumped off the ground, pockets stuffed with whole and torn dollar bills, and dashed for the bank door. Part of the greedy crowd tried to lock the doors but the angry ones outside broke the windows and set off the alarms. The vice president soon found himself dazed and beaten with a few torn dollars in his hand propped against the curb and at a total loss. A speeding malicious car roared by and hit the banker, rolling him out into the middle of the street still clutching the torn bills.

The random chaos of the city, the mixture of unrestraint, violence, and madness resembled some kind of a horrible Mardi Gras as throngs of citizens paraded around in fancy clothes raided from the poshest of boutiques. Expensive radios and tape players blared out all manner of music as people danced in the streets, drunk and eating any stolen cuisine without even the slightest feeling of restraint.

In the neighborhood on the edge of the Watts area, one outspoken young man in his late twenties, with a very developed physique, addressed a small group on a merchandise strewn sidewalk. They had pockets full of money taken from an over-turned Brinks truck, and the group was fired up ready for more action.

"Hey, I know where this sharp Jaguar is," the street man boldly stated. "If there's anything I've wanted all my life, it's a jag! And if there was ever a chance to get it, now is the time. Come on, you guys. Let's go on a spree. No holds barred. Let's pull out all the stops!"

"Yeah," one of the other ones added. "Let's clean up the good pickings before these fools wake up. You'll get you a jag, and I'll get me a Benz!"

"And I'll rip me an Eldorado!" another one chimed in.

One at the tail end of the group was not thoroughly convinced. He was torn between what he felt in his heart and the aggressive actions of his companions.

"What about the thing?" he asked reluctantly.

"What thing?" the streetman asked roughly.

"You know," the timid one replied, "the overpast. Don't you think we should hang close to one of these shelters just in case something happens? You know. Just to play it safe."

"You stupid chump!" the streetman called out, "If you believe that crap you're just as dumb as the rest of these fools! That was the biggest scam the world has ever seen. That Messenger cat is probably out here in the streets getting his. Can't you see through that chump style game?"

"I don't know," came the reply of the timid one. "All that stuff he did, I don't know if anybody regular could pull that off."

The streetman grabbed the young man by the collar and pinned him to a brick wall.

"Look, you hillbilly freak! You're either in or out! I got no time for Lilly livered punks!"

He then planted a knee in the reluctant one's groin, doubling him over as the turned with the gang and lead them up the block. They found an old Ford at the end of the next block with a door that had been hit and stripped off, and a serious dent in the front fender. One of the boys hotwired the car and streetman and his followers ganged in and headed on up the street, laughing and careening the cat onto a sidewalk.

They terrorized some stragglers hitting one and scattering a crowd that was gathered outside while looting an electronics store. The gang hit a strip of car dealerships and when they got to the gated-up Jaguar dealer, streetman hit the gas pedal and dove the old clunker straight through the metal gated window. He crashed the gate and all into a shiny new car on the sales floor as glass flew and the members of the group were thrown in every direction inside the Ford. There was a halting silence as one of the members of the group in the front seat sat slumped back unconscious and bleeding from a gaping head injury. Streetman; dazed, pulled himself out from the wheel and wandered out quickly coming to.

"You're crazy, Danny!" came a shout from one other member of the group, getting out of the back, also dazed but unhurt.

Streetman turned around addressing the group which emerged from the rear seat, "I got us here, didn't I?"

He began to brush the glass from his sleeves and shake himself off. He then held his hands out in presentation and looked around, "Well, here we are, boys. Take your pick."

The gang eyes gleamed at all the new cars on the showroom floor. Streetman ran over to one, a shiny sleek blue on black Jaguar El Leux.

"This one's mine!" he declared.

"What about Jeffrey?" one asked, pointing to the bleeding unconscious figure in the front seat.

"What can we do about that?" Streetman said, getting into the sleek new Jaguar, "Is anyone of you a doctor? I'm getting off in this jag. Any of you coming?"

A couple of the group unlocked and rolled up the wide entrance door and darted for the Jaguar.

"My Benz is next!" one said again, jumping in.

Two others stayed behind, helping Jeffrey out of the front seat while the Jaguar started up and sped out and up the block with some of the gang members screaming obscenities out of the window.

A group shelter had been set up in a commercial building in another part of the city. Fredia, an attractive sixteen-year-old, was engaged in a heated argument with her mother. Fredia had been patiently watching the people on the streets and secretly, she wanted to be out there experiencing the things she was seeing. Her heart had not been with the people in the shelter, but at the same time, under the will of her mother, she had gone along. The restless young lady turned the stool she was sitting on watching out the large picture window.

"Mom, please, I want to be outside. There are lots of other people out there."

"You shouldn't be concerned with those other people out there. You should stop looking out of the window. I want you to stay here!" her mother stated firmly.

Mrs. Johnson was an overweight, dark-haired woman who glowed with a warmth that only a mother could. Fredia looked away and brushed her soft-soled shoes against the window ledge.

"Mom, I only want to see what Nan and Tracy are doing. I'll come right back."

"Nancy and Tracy are doing whatever they are supposed to be doing. Whether it's good or bad, it only matters that you do what you're supposed to. That man, the Messenger, was a man of God."

Her mother looked up above her, "He told us to take this shelter and prepare for what is to come. I don't know what it might be, but always, you listen to the man of God. We will not budge from this spot until the overpast has come and we receive the sign. You stay put until it's over."

"Mrs. Johnson?" one of the directors came into the room and called out. "We're moving some cots and we could use your assistance."

Fredia's mother went straightway to help with the cots. When Fredia saw her mother was out of view, she eased her way over to the side door and slipped out. When she stepped outside. She closed her eyes and leaned against the wall taking in a deep breath. She looked up in the air and smiled at her newfound freedom. In an anxious chatter of fresh excitement, Fredia ran down the block taking in all of the destruction and somehow finding it fascinating. As she passed by the front of a window shattered liquor store, a drunk with a bottle of expensive scotch in one hand reached out to her but she outmaneuvered his reach pushing his arm aside easily and kept running freely along the boulevard. The streets were filled with looted cars, all manner of electronic gear, and jewelry. Men and women dressed in new expensive outfits walked down the streets arm and arm in drunken ecstasy.

Fredia's run slowed to a walk as she passed a furrier and saw a beautiful fur coat dangling off a mannequin. The front window was broken, and all of the other mannequins were in pieces but the looters, for one reason or another, had bypassed this coat. Having always wanted a fur, Fredia climbed into the window, careful not to touch the glass, and took the fur off the mannequin. She put it on and felt the luxurious softness of the pelt. It was slightly large but Fredia kept it, then jumping out of the window and heading on down the street.

She had not gone too far when she saw one of her school acquaintances sitting on the hood of a new car.

"Hey, Fredia," Janet energetically called out. "What's happening? I see you finally got hip and came out."

"Hi, Janet," Fredia greeted, eyes flashing at the new car. "I see you certainly have things hopping."

"Yeah, for sure," Janet acknowledged the admiring glare. "I left my mom yesterday. That old bag is really out of it. She said I had to stay in that stuffy old church and wait. Well, I said that's crap. I'm for what's happening!" Fredia laughed.

"Hey, listen Fredia, I want you to meet a couple of guys."

Janet kicked the fender and the head of a young handsome football player rose out of the front seat, "You know Chris."

Chris looked at Fredia leeringly. Fredia smiled.

Around from behind, another youth grabbed Janet by the waist and leaned her over, kissing her and grabbing her legs. Janet laughed and pulled her forward.

"Cut it out, Jermone," she cooed. "Fredia, this is Jerome. Jerome, this is Fredia."

"Well," Jerome smiled, almost chiding. "What have we here?"

Chris got out of the car and walked up, putting his arm around Fredia.

"How about a little MJ?" he smiled, holding up a couple of joints.

"Well, Merry Christman."

Janet giggled as Chris put the two in his mouth lighting up both, handing one to Janet and one to Fredia.

Janet took a drag and held in the smoke, coughing and laughing at the same time.

"What do you think about this Messenger junk?" she asked.

"I think it's a joke," Chris said.

"I don't know what to think," Fredia said. "My mom says it was certain to come sooner or later. That the world was too evil to continue as it is."

"Take a hit and pass it," Jerome said to Fredia. "It's gonna burn out."

Fredia closed her eyes and took a drag. She could hardly hold the first one in and coughed, making the others laugh, but the second puff was easier to take.

Chris began to whiff the perfume in Fredia's hair. He brushed his lips across the back of her neck.

"I know one thing that will always remain as it is…" he whispered.

Fredia raised her shoulders under Chris's touch. Chills ran through her as he put his arms on her shoulders. She looked into his soft brown eyes from over her shoulder and the sudden urge to kiss him clasped them into a long warm embrace. Chris looked up at Janet and Jerome who were giggling jokingly and winked at the two.

In a large church in the Hollywood area, Reverend Jacobs walked around and spoke words of comfort and encouragement to the flock of people that had taken refuge in his church building. Reverend Jacobs was a tall, solidly build man with roving deep-set eyes and a wave of deep brown hair which he combed to the side in a parted manner.

A sharply dressed street hustler came into the church and looked over the group hovered together on the benches and on the steps of the church pulpit area. There was a mixture of reverence and at the same time, disdain, in his eyes as the hustler made his way quietly to the front of the church in the reverend's direction. Reverend Jacobs looked nervously at his flock and at the hustler approaching him.

He gestured in an overly friendly manner careful that those watching and heard him, "Ah! Brother TJ. Happy to you, my son. Step into my office and maybe I can help you with your problem."

The reverend then finished up what he was doing and nervously hurried back to his office. He was watched suspiciously by many of the elders who observed his cautious behavior.

"I told you never to come to the church!" he gruffly said in a hushed manner once he closed the door.

"What else am I supposed to do, man?" the hustler commented. "You ain't leaving this place."

"I can't leave. I got an image to consider."

The reverend opened a bottom drawer and pulled out a fifth of bourbon which was half empty. He opened it and took a swig of the liquid showing a bitter weary face as the drink went down. He sat the bottle on the desk, holding on to it, and looked up at the hustler.

"You don't know what it's like," the minister confided, "having to keep up under the probing eyes of old ladies with nothing else to do."

He took another drink of the bourbon and capped it, putting it back into the drawer.

"Did you get the stuff?"

"Man, I ran across some stuff you never have seen before. Most of the things I set you up with earlier was all twelve carrots. This is bloodstone, tigers' eye, and manmade emerald set all in fourteen carrots!"

The hustler pulled from his coat a hand full of jewels in a gold setting. Broaches, necklaces, bracelets, chains; all beautifully hand finished.

The reverend took a couple of the broaches and held them up to the light. He smiled as he looked upon the rare beauty of them. As he looked lovingly at them, as if in wonder, the hustler pulled out a small black cashmere box.

"Dig this," he said, opening the box slowly.

As he did, Reverend Jacob's eyes widened. He dropped the broaches on his desk and took the box. Out of it, he raised up a black pearl.

"Cultured?" he asked, eyes still wide.

"Nope," the hustler said proudly, "natural."

The minister had to hold his breath from gasping at the thought of it. "How did you arrange this?" he asked.

"I do have some connections," the hustler bragged.

The minister smiled broadly and got a key out from a hidden side of his desk. He opened a thin drawer above the wide flat one at the top of the desk and removed an envelope from it.

"You have done well, my friend," the reverend said with satisfaction as he pressed the envelope on the hustler.

The hustler counted the money quickly and smiled as he placed it in the upper pocket just inside his jacket lapel.

"We try to please," the hustler said, opening the door to leave the office.

The two of them stepped out into the church, and the reverend then called out most conspicuously as the hustler made his way for the exit.

"So happy I could be of help to you, brother."

Lying down on the fur coat with Chris on top of her, Fredia let her emotions run with the kisses and artful touches of the experienced young men. She felt a twinge of guilt emerge now and then, but the passion of the uninhibited indulgence was enough to over-ride it and she threw herself deeper into the pleasure of their embrace.

Janet and Jerome were not buzzed by the marijuana and uncapped a couple of beers retrieved from the trunk of the car. They laughed and joked between kisses about any number of things they found funny at the time. Jerome was getting more and more intoxicated by the combination of marijuana and beer, and he became noticeably more wobbly in his manner.

"Hey!" he stated, waving his finger pointing at the sky almost in a drunken stupor. "Am I just drunk, or is the sky getting funny?"

Janet laughed at what seemed like a joke. She looked up at the sky and something struck her odd about it too. Something foreboding. For a passing instant, she got the slightest momentary feeling of fear.

"The sky!" she yelled out trying to joke her way out. "The sky is falling!"

The two of them laughed loudly and Janet took another swig off of Jerome's can of beer.

Fredia heard the joking and something in her sounded an alarm. She rose up and Chris was suddenly pushed to the side of the car seat.

"What's wrong, baby?" he asked, almost in irritation.

"The sky?" Fredia said, as if to herself. She forced her way past Chris and got out of the car while Chris, in bewilderment, got out and questioned behind her.

"The sky!" Fredia exclaimed, this time even louder. "It's getting darker."

"Darker? What are you talking about?" Charis said. He looked at a very expensive watch on his wrist. "It's only two o'clock. What are you talking about?"

"I don't know," Fredia said nervously looking at thc sky. "I gotta go."

"What?" Chris stated angrily.

Janet and Jerome laughed, and Jerome again leaned Janet back all the way on the car hood, angling his body on top of hers in a drunken giddy passionate kiss.

Grabbing her fur coat and not looking back, Fredia ran off in the direction of her shelter.

At the same time, coming up the block, was a group of young men with two women at the head of the pack. One carried a lard expensive tape player on her shoulder blaring out music. The group danced with each other and one younger male with a revolver randomly shot it off as the whim hit him between jerking movements.

"It looks like it going to rain," the other woman commented with casual concern.

"All of sudden it's getting colder,"

"Let it rain!"

A streetman came up behind the woman and put his arm around her.

"I got me a new Jaguar, loads of money…"

He then kissed the woman quickly and squarely on the lips, "And a fine foxy mama in my corner. Who cares if it rains?"

He turned around and yelled out, "Ain't that right, boys?"

"Ya-hoo!" yelled the youngest one as he shot the pistol off into the air and the whole group kept on partying down the street. The party group passed and an intoxicated middle-aged man with a sledgehammer who was beating in the fenders, the hood, and the windows of a large automobile.

"I always wanted to do in this gas-destroyer!" the angry man screamed as he pounded away with all his might. As the partying group came to pass, the man took a swing at one of the members, hitting one squarely in the back with the hammer. The younger member with the pistol turned and shot the man with the hammer and the group kept dancing on down the street.

The sky kept getting darker as Fredia ran past this group en route to her sanctuary. Seeing the darkness mount, terror grew in her eyes as she felt the impending doom.

"I can make it!" she screamed. "I've got to make it!"

Tears began to run down her face as she ran furiously. A man leaning against a lamp post grabbed her, catching her one arm as she came past.

"Slow down, little girl," he stated calmly. His eyes had an insane look in them, and his hair was mussed and out of place.

"Everything is going to be alright," he said maniacally. "I think the grass is going to grow. Do you like the nice green grass?"

"Let me go! Let me go!" Fredia screamed as she scratched him until she broke free. She shook her head, stammering backward away from the maddened figure, and began running again for the shelter.

The sky oozed a grayish doom when instantly, every door slammed shut and locked itself. The clicking sounds could be heard at once and in succession, omnipresent sound like the clicking of unloading shotgun shells. The walls inside of the cross secured buildings tighten and squeak, and the sky outside totally dimmed the atmosphere.

The enveloping darkness waxed heavy on the souls of those who were on the outside of the shelters. Everyone who had not believed began to feel the recompense for their unfaithfulness. Screams and moans were uttered from the throats of the masses left outside. On the inside of the sanctuaries, many of the people knelt and prayed for mercy.

Fredia's mother waited with her forehead pressed to the window and searched amongst the outsiders she could see scurrying in bewilderment for her daughter. Tears streamed down her face as she cried to herself.

"My baby. My little baby. I told you, Fredia…not to go out! Please! My baby. Oh, let her come back. Please hurry!"

Fredia was running tiredly in the thickness and was only yards away from the sanctuary.

"Fredia!" her mother shrieked upon seeing her image.

She ran to the front door and pulled on it. But the door would not open. She dropped to her knees and pleaded.

"Somebody, help me! Please, help Fredia. Tell me it's not too late! Oh, please don't let her die!"

Again, only this time more frantically, her mother pulled on the door but to no avail.

Fredia pounded on the window outside, her face wet with tears and her eyes wide with fear. The director rushed into the room and called out to her mother.

"Get away from the door! It's too late. It's too late!"

Mrs. Johnson could not hear him. She continued to pull and kick on the door hysterically. As Fredia's raps on the window faded, becoming fainter and fainter, her mother began to sob loudly.

"My baby! Oh, my little baby! She was so young. Oh, please! Please!"

A couple of caretakers assigned in the group tried to pull her away from the door, but Mrs. Johnson fought them. She looked out at the window and by now could barely see her daughter. She only saw faint outlines of the young girl and was driven even stronger by the hope. She broke free of the caretakers and heaved a good-sized wooden chair-throwing it against the picture window. The article bounced off the glass resounding like a tightly skinned drum. The window wasn't so much as scratched.

The futility of her efforts was beginning to mount upon her and after more tugs, at the door, Mrs. Johnson fell to a heap on the floor near the door. She was nearly limp. The woman sobbed in extreme regret and could not be consoled. Some of the older women were finally able to help her up and walked her over to a resting cot in the next room.

Outside, a thick black fog came over all of the refuge areas where crosses on all four corners were in place. No one could see out who was inside of the shelters and no one outside could see into them. The lost and the faithless banged on the doors and windows of the sanctuaries, and stumbled in the darkness and fog that had enveloped them. The pain and the guilt for the things which they had done filled their hearts and they pleaded to those inside for one final chance. Many of the ones who had stolen money or jewels sensed their utter uselessness and threw them away. Some tried to snatch the crosses made of the various materials from the corners of the sanctuaries but burned their hands whenever they touched them. At a corner of the commercial building, a desperate man wrapped his shirt around his hand and tried to take one of the secured crosses off, but the shirt caught on fire and was consumed rapidly.

The buildings that were not secured with crosses were open and many of the outsiders ran into them to get out of the streets, but the thick black fog was present inside of these structures. The darkness reached a pitch which was almost impenetrable and as it did, the moans of fear intensified almost to a maximum. The outsiders screamed for help and scratched at the walls and doors of the sanctuaries but could not be satisfied. They ran through the streets, bumping blindly into objects and other people. They clutched hold of each other, but they could not be comforted. Although those inside heard the cries for help, they could not open their refuge areas. It seemed that those who had heeded the call of the Messenger were spared the awesome fate of those who did not listen.

Reverend Jacobs stood in the pulpit, casually glancing through some books while his congregation and others under his care were diligently praying for their relatives and loved ones. One elder woman in the far corner of the church began to rock back and forth, intently writhing at the sounds she heard outside. The tightening walls squeaked and plaster at the corners fell to the floor. There were moans and faint scratches and clawing at the doors and windows.

"My boy!" the hysterical elder woman began to scream, "my boy's out there." The reverend looked up from his reading at the commotion in the back of the church. Some of the other church members went to the woman's aid and comfort.

"What's wrong with her?" the reverend demanded.

One of the deacons of the church stood up and hesitantly addressed the minister.

"Ah, Reverend," he said, rather reluctantly. "Some of our loved ones are out there. I have a daughter."

"Yes, Reverend," one of the other members added. "My father is out there."

"All of my children are in the darkness," came still another voice from the back of the church.

The minister closed his book and rubbed his forehead. "Why does it always have to be me?" he complained. The reverend stood there, thinking for a moment. He then went to a closet near his office and gathered from it a large sledgehammer and two large crowbars.

Walking briskly to the front entrance, Reverend signaled a couple of the stronger young men in the congregation with him. The trio proceeded to pound on the doors and use the crowbars in an attempt to open them. It was like pounding on steel.

"No! No!" came the voice of one of the elder men rushing to the front area. "Don't do that. Please, Reverend Jacobs. Don't let what's out there inside! It's not God's will. We must not bring the fats of the unfaithful upon ourselves."

Other members stood up, intoning the three to cease. Not paying attention, the reverend grew frustrated with the two young members trying to get the doors open.

"Please, Reverend?" the elder, along with certain other members, continued to plead.

"I don't want to hear that," the reverend said, more out of frustration in not getting the doors open than anything. Breathing heavily, he threw the hammer down on the floor.

"That's enough, fellows," he said, turning to the congregation which was taken back by his callous attitude.

"I think we should all rest and pray."

He then offered in a somewhat conciliatory manner, "I can't get the busted thing open anyway."

He walked up to the front of the church with all eyes on him and dropped on his knees, knowing he was being watched by all. He started out praying and was joined a few at a time by his flock.

Outside, the lost ones continued to pound and scratch on the doors, pleading for help, but their pleads could not be aided. Certain members of the congregation cringed as the please grew weaker and less frequent.

The Kellys family sat on their living room floor close to each other on the comfort of the blankets and pillows which had been their resting spots for the past two days. The couple prayed and read the Bible while Linda rested on her mother's lap. They did not know what was happening outside of their sanctuary, but they were determined to remain obedient to the end. Linda frequently had to be comforted because of the intermittent explosions and screams she heard in the night. Ann stroked her pretty brown hair and read to her, in soft tones. As the Kellys sat in vigilance, there was a soft knock at the door.

"Charles." A voice struggled from the front door.

Ann was the first to make it out, "Kurt?"

Charles rose up alertly and looked at the front door in surprise and fear.

"Let me in, Ann. Ann, it's us!" Jennifer screamed.

The voice of Jennifer cut straight to Ann's heart. She closed her eyes and gripped the book she was holding to her chest.

"Linda! Linda! Mister Kelly, open the door. Let us in."

Linda rose up quickly and looked over to the front door at the sound of Tommy's voice. Ann reached for her, but she darted up just ahead of Ann's reach. She ran frantically for the front door in her innocence to aid Tommy.

"No!" Charles called out as she lunged forward and caught his daughter and held her tightly. She fought to want to get at the door and Ann, face wet with tears, swiftly went over to comfort her daughter.

"It's alright, baby," Ann pleaded to rub back Linda's hair.

"I want to, Linda," Charles stammered, trying to choke back the tears, "but we can't."

"Please let us in. We've suffered enough!" Kurt pleaded.

"Let the baby in," Jennifer mournfully added.

Under Charles's guidance, the Kellys family returned to their resting places. There was not the way they could open the door even if they had wanted to. The warnings had gone forth. Everyone had had a change. From the time of its inception. Whatever was to happen could not be changed anymore.

Ann finally succeeded in claiming Linda. The family wrapped themselves in the blankets on the floor and again began to pray for all those who were outside, and for those of the faithful. The pleas at their front door faded off as the Kellys continued their night benediction.

As the night went on, explosions and the sounds of buildings falling apart could be heard all over the city by those secured in their sanctuaries. The outsiders moaned and wretched before dropping lifeless. Other victims fell through store windows still clutching stolen items in their grasp. There were piles of clothing everywhere. Large amounts of lifeless blowing clothes were all around the sanctuaries, the only evidence of the pleading loss. The disobedient outsiders, men, women, and children faded away to dust, and the wind blew their ashes out into the Pacific Ocean.

Reverend Jacobs stayed up late that night, reading by a small light in his pulpit long after the members of his congregation one by one had faded off, after a long distressing night, into slumber. The reverend looked out at the sleeping members and scoffed to himself. He'd been a pastor of the church for two years and he had grown tired of the board meetings, and budgetary accounting. This thing, whatever it was, had come not a moment too soon. He had cashed in on all the hysteria caused by the disturbance the Messenger had cause, and soon he would reap the benefits.

Walking back to his office, he took a seat behind his large mahogany desk. Once again, he pulled out a hidden key and unlocked a large flat drawer at the top of the desk. Pulling it back, it revealed wads of money and a smattering of jewelry, gold, and silver. He smiled broadly upon viewing his hidden treasure. He didn't know what was happening to the people outside, but he felt secure. He had taken advantage of the situation, gambled his reputation, stuck it out with his parishioners, and won. *Now*, he thought, *he'd be able to reap the benefits of his own cleverness.* Putting his hands behind his head, he leaned back in his chair and smiled, dreaming of vacationing in Florida and the Bahamas, leaving his despised job behind him.

Suddenly and rapidly, he felt a tingling feeling in the center of his chest. The tingling feeling swiftly turned to a burning sensation which quickly grew more intense. The pain gripped him, and he grabbed at his chest, falling to the floor. He began to lose his breath, and he clutched at his throat in dire agony. In attempted gasps for air, Reverend Jacobs rolled over on his back and smoke began to emanate from a cavity which had formed in his chest.

"Help me, somebody," he whispered in suffocation.

His reach grabbed the floor and the Reverend felt an instant heat sizzle away from his toes, up his legs, and engulf his entire body.

Early the next morning, there was silence throughout the church. An elder churchwoman rocked silently, tears flooded in her eyes, in a chair outside of the minister's office. As other members stirred and awoke, one of the deacons in yawning noticed the woman rocking silently on the chair.

"Martha?" he called out softly, with concern. "Martha, what's wrong? Where's Reverend Jacobs?"

Other members looked around the church in wonderment, some just waking up. Martha said nothing but pointed silently to the minister's office. The deacon went forward with a couple of the congregation. When the small group entered the office, they found only a pile of clothes on the floor and the pile of money and jewelry on the pastor's desk. One of the women turned her head quickly and was consoled by her brother who had gone in with the group.

"My husband!" A yell came from the main body, "Where's my husband? He's gone!"

The group scurried out of the office and found the woman searching through a smattering of clothes on the floor. She began crying as she held up his jacket to her face to smother the tears. Upon doing so, a small handkerchief rolled out of one pocket filled with stolen items. The members of the faithful looked on in amazement. Others of the church were gone as well. It seemed that all of the unbelievers and hypocrites inside of the sanctuaries had vanished as those of the outsiders.

Chapter 14
Aftermath

Waves rushed to the shores of the sandy beaches on the Spanish coast. The warm air blew calmly from the trade winds of the Mediterranean Sea. In the sky above, flocks of honking geese flew eastward in the morning sky. All the way up the coasts of Western Europe, the surviving believers emerged from their shelters and gazed in wonder at the new world around them. The remaining people in the populous industrial centers in the interior of Europe also came forth to view a unique morning skyline, unlike any they had ever seen before.

Across the face of Russia and indeed the entire Asian continent, the outflowing masses of the faithful studied in amazement about them. Buildings and monuments that had existed for centuries were gone. There was a distinct stillness in the air that was smoothly peaceful. Down through the Mideastern states off the coast of Northern Africa and deep into the furthest most reaches of the vast continent, the people who believed departed from their shelters to see the nature around them in its greenest form. The natural wonders had been enhanced, and bright men, women, and children who emerged walked out silently and beheld the beauty of the changes. In South and Central America, entire families who had waited and prayed together in the numerous churches which tended the populations were astonished by the difference they saw. In Australia and on the island nations of the world, people protected by the cross secured shelters sighed in joyful relief. The whole Earth had experienced a transformation, and as the preserved inhabitants wandered out and viewed it, there was almost universal jubilation.

Enormous changes had occurred throughout North America. All of the major cities and ports were radically different. Places that once stood even as monuments to wickedness and greed were gone. Evil networks that had taken decades to build were wiped from the face of the Earth.

In Los Angeles, as the protected stepped out of their shelters; they were amazed by what had transpired. Much of the technology of the giant urban metropolis had been destroyed. Clothes of all shapes and sizes blew in the winds, the only remnants of the unfaithful and a reminder of their unbelief. Those who were true believers praised God. They openly rejoiced at the new beginning. The air smelled freshly clean because the pollution and smog which had hovered over Los Angeles for years was gone.

The buildings which remained untouched stood out immaculately. The park areas appeared greener and more alive than they had ever seemed before. The litter and paper which had blown in the streets was gone, and the very streets themselves looked as if they'd been scrubbed with very fine brushed until every square micro-inch was spotless.

Flocks of geese honked loudly overhead flying easterly, and those who saw the very blue clear morning sky breathed deeply, inhaling the clean crisp air. The wild dogs, rats, and other menacing creatures that had roamed the city were no more. The dope dispensing outlets were leveled.

In what was once the Hollywood district, a group of unsure but fearing believers cautiously ventured out on a secured church's steps. A very careful member of the group at the back left the door open. He wanted an escape route in case the group had to make a hasty retreat. The group, sticking close together, looked over the destruction and the very pleasant state of things which had taken their place. An exhilarating flash rushed through them, but still uncertain, they made a further survey of their newfound environment.

They came upon an open field and noticed a lone trash dumpster setting there in the middle of the field. The dumpster was the only remnant on a site upon which had stood several very large old gray stone buildings. The group stood looking at the large area of debris strewn land. They marveled at the total emptiness of a spot which only a few days ago had been fully occupied. As they stirred in amazement, their attention was drawn by a slow creaking noise coming from the dumpster. All movement stopped and the group stood frozen in their tracks. The dumpster so slowly rose as the squeaking metal sound emanated from the shadow of the opening door. Eyes widened with fear, the group huddled closer together until it flipped all the way back. Out of it raised the head of a once intoxicated bum who had prepared in faith. The sudden light in his eyes made him wince, and the bristly character behaved as if he didn't know where he was.

There was a simultaneous sigh of relief from the group who relaxed at the sight of the bum, some chuckled openly. The bum slowly climbed out of the dumpster still trying to get his bearings. He stood wobbly and was startled by the vacant lots and the absence of buildings that had been there before he climbed into the dumpster.

At their brownstone home in the former Pasadena suburb of Los Angeles, the Kellys family stretched out on the living-room floor, resting comfortably after a long night of vigilance. Charles Kellys embraced his wife in a peaceful calm slumber while Linda laid relaxing near her parents, humming a pleasant melody and holding up to view a small Indian doll from her collection.

A small ray of sunlight streamed through a shutter and down to the floor where the Kellys rested. Linda smiled and put her doll down beside her. She then got up and followed the ray of light to the shutter, tilting one slat of the shutter upward. She looked out and smiled at the sun-drenched clear blue sky.

Charles, aroused by the faint rustlings of his daughter, opened one eye and then both, as he shifted position from Ann. Ann woke up abruptly, stirred by Charles's motion, stretching putting a hand over her yawn. Charles turned his head and saw Linda gazing and smiling out of the slightly raised blinds.

"Mama, I think it's over," Linda said, turning to look at her parents.

Charles's eyes widened, and his mouth dropped as he heard the words from his daughter. Ann was immediately filled with excitement at what she heard.

"Oh, Linda!" Ann exclaimed, holding her arms out.

Linda ran over to Ann with tears of joy in her eyes. Charles, in uncontrollable euphoria, hugged both of them.

"It's over, Mama," Linda said again, this time with greater firmness in her voice, "It's finally over."

Charles said nothing but hugged the two of them tighter. The healing of his daughter's voice, that she could speak, cut to his heart like a dagger. Charles closes his eyes tightly and tears streamed down his face. He couldn't find words to express his thanks to God. That his family was well, and that his daughter, miraculously, could speak.

The family, in refreshed newness, stood up together. Ann continued to look at and embrace Linda. Charles raised his head back, trying to fathom the miracle.

"Thank you," he whispered, smiling with greater joy than he could express. He then looked at his little girl.

They walked toward the door. Ann held Linda around the shoulders, Linda held on to her mother. On the floor at their feet was the one ray of light peeking in through the blinds. It was awesome yet wonderful to even think what the changes were that might lay ahead for them.

Charles removed the bracing chair at the front door. He unlocked the various locks and put his hand on the knob. Looking at his wife with anticipation, she extended out and clasped Charles's extended hand, stepping next to him. Once again with his arm around his family, Charles opened the door slowly to the most beautiful scene he'd ever beheld. The bright sunlight fell upon the family and past the threshold into the house. There was a peaceful warm breeze that filled up their senses, all the colors were brighter, and the atmosphere was crisp and clean and of the most beautiful. Off beyond the fragrant landscape, above all the trees, spanning from horizon to horizon, the Kelly family viewed the sight of a most glorious rainbow.

The End

www.ingramcontent.com/pod-product-compliance
Lightning Source LLC
Chambersburg PA
CBHW061733050726
47598CB00002B/459